THE SAGA OF ARROW-ODD

Edited by Gavin Chappell

Thor's Stone Press

Copyright © 2014 Gavin Chappell

All rights reserved

The characters and events portrayed in this book are fictitious. Any similarity to real persons, living or dead, is coincidental and not intended by the author.

No part of this book may be reproduced, or stored in a retrieval system, or transmitted in any form or by any means, electronic, mechanical, photocopying, recording, or otherwise, without express written permission of the publisher.

Paperback ISBN: 9798863846675

THE SAGA OF ARROW-ODD

If Norse saga has an equivalent of the *Odyssey*, then it must be *The Saga of Arrow-Odd*, a lengthy tale of a man blessed or cursed (much like Norna-Gest) with an unusually long life, in which he wanders, at times aimlessly, across the world of Viking mythology. Although in that respect it resembles the *Odyssey*, the story of Odd also has parallels with that classical poem's prequel, the *Iliad*, in that its doomed protagonist also participates in the greatest conflict to trouble the legendary, prehistoric Scandinavian world, the Bravic War.

However, for reasons unknown, possibly artistic, the author of the longer saga that has come down to us misses out Odd's involvement in this terrible war, although it appears in Saxo Grammaticus' *Gest Danorum* and the *Fragment of a Saga of Some Kings of the North*. Presumably, the author thought it a little bit too much, what with three hundred years of adventuring across the northern world; the curse (or blessing) of an inevitable death (reminiscent of Oedipus' fate in Greek myth, although Odd does a far better job, though still tragically inevitable, of avoiding it); not to mention a long-running feud with an even more invulnerable enemy: Ogmund Tussock, half-man, half-wraith, created by the powers of evil to avenge Odd's early raid on the mysterious world of Bjarmaland.

It is a long and terrible voyage that intersects with several other sagas, some of them previously translated, such as *The Saga of Hervor and Heidrek*, others still to be produced. Along the way, Arrow-Odd, son of Grim Hairy-cheek, son of Ketil Trout, encounters many foes in the worlds of men – Ireland, Russia, Greece, and Syria – and elsewhere. He meets the giants of Norse myth and the monsters of the St Brendan saga, scorns the sorcery of his Scandinavian homeland, converts to Christianity in Aquitania (without agreeing to do more than pay lip service), and outlives his friends and foes (other than Ogmund) until he has little left to do other than meet his inevitable fate.

CHAPTER ONE

There was a man named Grim who was called Hairycheek. He was so called because when he was born, he had an odd quirk; when Ketil Trout, father of Grim, and Hrafnhild Bruni's daughter went to bed together, as has already been mentioned, her father spread a hide over them because he had invited some Lapps there, and during the night Hrafnhild looked out from under the hide and saw one Lapp who was exceedingly hairy. And it was then that Grim got his mark; people think that he was begotten at that moment. Grim lived at Hrafnista. He was a wealthy man and powerful throughout Halogaland and elsewhere. He was married, and Lofthaena was his wife. She was the daughter of Lord Harald from the Vik in the east.

One summer, after the death of Harald, his brother in law, Grim made a journey eastwards to the Vik where he had much property. When Lofthaena knew of this, she asked to go with him, but Grim said that it could not be, - 'because you are expecting.'

'I will not be happy,' she said, 'unless I go.' Grim loved her dearly, and he let things go her way.

She was very good-looking and in everything she did she was the cleverest woman in Norway. They fitted themselves out lavishly.

Grim sailed with two ships out from Hrafnista eastwards to Vik. But when they came to the country named Berurjod, Lofthaena said that she wanted them to reef sails because she could feel her labour starting, and so it was done, the ships made for land. A man named Ingjald lived there. He was married and had a son with his wife, a handsome youth called Asmund. And when they came ashore, they sent to the farm to tell Ingjald that Grim had come to the country with his wife. Then Ingjald had horses hitched to a cart and went to them himself and offered them all the hospitality they needed, and whatever they would receive. Then they went home to the farm of Ingjald. Lofthaena was shown to the women's house, but Grim was led into the hall and set on the high-seat, and Ingjald thought nothing he could do too much to show respect to Grim's group. But Lofthaena's labour pangs grew until she was delivered of a young boy, and the women who took care of him had never seen such a fine child. Lofthaena looked at the boy and said, 'Carry him to his father. He should name the child,' and so it was done. The boy was sprinkled with water and given the name Odd. There they stayed three nights. Lofthaena told Grim that she was ready to go, and Grim told Ingjald that he wanted to leave.

'It occurs to me,' said Ingjald, 'that I would like to get a sign of your respect from you.'

'That's well deserved,' said Grim, 'so choose your own reward, because I have no lack of treasure to pay you.'

'I have enough treasure,' said Ingjald. 'Then you must accept something else,' said Grim. 'I offer to become your son's foster father,' said Ingjald. 'I do not know,' said Grim, 'how Lofthaena will take that.' But she replied: 'I suggest you accept it, because it's a good offer.'

Then they were led to their ships, but Odd stayed behind at Berurjod. They took up their journey again, so that they arrived eastwards in the Vik, and they stayed as long as they thought necessary. Then they prepared to sail away from there, and they had a good wind until they came to Berurjod. Grim told his men to reef sails. 'Why should we not go on with our voyage?' said Lofthaena. 'I thought,' said Grim, 'that you would like to see your son.'

'I looked at him,' she said, 'before we separated, and it seemed to me that he had little love in his eyes for Hrafnista men, and so we will go on our way,' she said.

Now Grim returned home to Hrafnista and settled on his estate, but Odd grew up at Berurjod with Asmund. Odd was good at all the accomplishments of the time. Asmund followed him in all respects. Odd was very good-looking and smarter than other men.

Odd and Asmund became sworn brothers. They practiced archery every day, or swimming. No one was equal to Odd in any accomplishments. Odd would not play games like other people. Asmund always followed him. In all things Ingjald preferred Odd to Asmund.

Odd had every skilful man he found make him arrows. He did not take good care of them, and they lay around in people's way on seats and benches. Many were hurt by them, when people came in after dark and sat down. This one thing was agreed, that it made Odd unpopular. Men told Ingjald that he should talk to Odd about this. Ingjald met with Odd one day. 'There is one thing,' said Ingjald, 'foster-son, that makes you unpopular.'

'What is that?' said Odd. 'You do not take care of your arrows like other people,' said Ingjald. 'I think you could blame me for it,' said Odd, 'if you had given me something to keep them in.'

'I shall get you,' said Ingjald, 'what you want.'

'I think,' said Odd, 'that you will not get it.'

'It will not be so,' said Ingjald. 'You have a black three-year-old goat,' said Odd. 'Have him killed and skinned whole with both horns and hoofs.' And it was done as Odd asked, and he was brought the skin-bag when it was ready. Then he gathered all his arrows into it, and did not stop until the skin-bag was full. He had much larger arrows, and more of them, than other people. He had a bow to match.

Odd wore a scarlet robe every day, and had an embroidered gold headband round his brow. He had his quiver with him wherever he went. Odd did not make sacrifices, because he believed in his might and main, and Asmund did as he did, but Ingjald was a great man for sacrifices. The sworn brothers, Odd and Asmund, often rowed out from the land together.

CHAPTER TWO

There was a woman named Heid. She was a seeress and a witch and knew how to predict the future with her wisdom. She went to banquets and told people how the winter would go and their fortunes. She had with her fifteen young men and fifteen girls. She was at a banquet not far away from Ingjald. One morning Ingjald was up early. He went to where Odd and Asmund rested, and said: 'I will send you both from the house today,' he said. 'Where will we go?' said Odd. 'You shall invite here the seeress, because we have now prepared a feast,' said Ingjald. 'I will not do that,' said Odd, 'and you will fall out of my favour if she comes here.'

'You must go, Asmund,' said Ingjald, 'because I expect you to.'

'I will do something,' said Odd, 'that will seem to you no better than this seems to me now.'

Asmund went and invited the seeress there, and she promised to come and came up with her following, and Ingjald went to meet her with all his men and invited her into his house. They had prepared auguries to be carried out that night. And when people had enough to eat, they went to sleep, but the seeress went to her night-time ritual with her followers. Ingjald came to her in the morning and asked what had been the result of the auguries. 'I think,' she said, 'that I have learned all you wish to know.'

'Then everyone shall go to their seats,' said Ingjald, 'and hear your words.' Ingjald was the first man to go to her. 'It is well, Ingjald,' she said, 'that you have come here. I can tell you that you shall live here until old age with great dignity and respect, and this may be much welcomed by all your friends.' Then Ingjald went off, and Asmund came. 'It is well,' said Heid, 'that you have come here, Asmund, for your honour and dignity will go around the world. You will not wrestle with old age, but you will be thought a good fellow and a great warrior wherever you are.' Asmund went to his seat, and everybody else went to the spaewife, and she told each of them their fortunes, and they were all well satisfied with their lot. Then she predicted the winter, and many other things that no one knew before. Ingjald thanked her for her predictions. 'Has everyone come here, those who are within the court?' she said. 'I think now almost everyone,' said Ingjald. 'What lies on the bench over there?' said the seeress. 'A cloak is lying there,' said Ingjald. 'I think it stirs sometimes, when I look,' she said. Then he sat up, who was lying there, and he began to speak and said: 'That's right, you thought that this is a man, because it is a man, and what he wants is for you to be quiet at once and babble not about my future, because I do not believe what you say.' Odd had a rod in his hand and said: 'I will hit you on the nose with this, if you prophesy at all about my future.' She said, 'I will still speak, and you will hear.' Then poetry came to her lips:

'Awe me not,

Odd of Jaederen,

With that rod,

Although we row.

This story will hold true,

Said by the seeress.

She knows beforehand

All men's fate.

You will not swim

Wide firths,

Nor go a long way

Over lands and bays,

Though the water will well

And wash over you,

You will burn

Here, at Berurjod.

Venom-filled snake

Shall sting you

From the ancient

Skull of Faxi.

The adder will bite

From below your foot,

When you are terribly

Old, my lord.

'This is to say, Odd,' she said, 'You may find it good to know that you are destined to live much longer than others. You shall live to be three hundred years old, and go from land to land, and always seem the greatest there, where you go. Your reputation will go around the world, but travel as far as you may, you'll die here, in Berurjod. The horse that is standing in the stable, black-maned and grey, Faxi, his skull will be your death.'

'You make the worst prophecies of any old woman,' said Odd. He jumped up as she said this and brought the rod down on her nose so hard that blood dripped on the ground. 'Take my belongings,' said the seeress, 'and I will go away from here, because I have never been treated like this before, that I was beaten.'

'Do not do that,' said Ingjald, 'for there's recompense for every ill, and you will stay here for three nights and get good gifts.' She took the presents, but she went away from the feast.[1]

CHAPTER THREE

After this Odd told Asmund to come with him. They took Faxi and bridled him and led him behind them until they came to a valley. Here they dug a deep pit, until Odd had a struggle to get out, and then they killed Faxi and dropped him down into the pit, and Odd and Asmund brought the biggest rocks they could carry and piled them on top of him and poured sand between every stone. They built a burial mound beneath which Faxi lay. When they had ended their work, Odd said: 'I think that I should say that trolls are involved if Faxi comes up, and I think I have now frustrated the fate that would be my death.'

They went home after that, and met Ingjald. 'I want a ship as a gift,' said Odd. 'Where will you go?' Ingjald said. 'I'll go, I think, from here,' said Odd, 'from Berurjod, and never come here as long as I live.'

'I do not want that,' said Ingjald, 'because then you would do what I think worst. What people do you want to have with you?'

'We two shall go, Asmund and I,' said Odd. 'I would like you to send Asmund back quickly,' said Ingjald. 'He shall not come back any more than I,' said Odd. 'This you do ill,' said Ingjald. 'I will do this, I think, that you will like worst, because you invited the seeress here, and you knew that I thought it the worst,' said Odd.

Now Odd and Asmund prepared to go and they went to Ingjald and bade him farewell and went to the ship and pushed it out; then they rowed away from the shore. 'Where will we go?' said Asmund. 'Is it not a good idea,' said Odd, 'to seek my kin in Hrafnista?' But when they came to some islands, Odd said, 'Hard work will our journey be if we have to row all the way north to Hrafnista; we will now know if I have any of our family luck. I am told that Ketil Trout hoisted his sail in calm weather. Now I shall try it and hoist the sails.' And when they were under sail they got a fair wind, so that they came to Hrafnista early in the day; they pulled up their boat on the beach and then went to the farm. Odd had no other weapon than the quiver of arrows he had on his back, and a bow in his hand. But when they came to the farm, a man stood outside and greeted them well, and then asked for their names. 'I'm not telling you,' said Odd. Odd then asked whether Grim was home. He said that he was at home. 'Then call him outside,' said Odd. The man went in and told Grim that two men had come, -

'and said that you should go out.'

'Why can they not come in?' Grim said, 'Ask them to enter.' Out he went and told them what had been said. 'You must go in a second time,' said Odd, 'and tell Grim that he must come out and meet us both.' He went and told Grim. 'What sort of men are these?' said Grim. 'These people are handsome and tall. One of them has an animal skin on his back.'

'What you say of these men means that the sworn brothers, Odd and Asmund, are come here.' Grim went out with all those who were inside, and welcomed Odd and Asmund. Grim invited them with him into the house, and they accepted.

And when they sat down, Odd asked after his relatives, Gudmund and Sigurd. Their kinship went so that Gudmund was brother of Odd, the son of Grim and Lofthaena, but Sigurd was the son of Grim's sister. They were promising men. 'They are to the north of the island and they plan to sail to Bjarmaland,' said Grim. 'Then I will see them,' said Odd. 'Well, I wish,' said Grim, 'that you stay here in the winter.'

'I will go first,' said Odd, 'and see them.' And then Grim went with him till they came to the island in the north. They had anchored there in two ships. Then their kinsman Odd called them to come ashore. They gave him a warm welcome, and when they heard the news, Odd said, 'Where have you decided to go?'

'To Bjarmaland,' said Gudmund. 'Asmund and I would go with you,' said Odd. But Gudmund had heard word of this, and said: 'There is no way, kinsman Odd, that you can come with us this summer. We two are now already equipped for our voyage, and you can come with me next summer, wherever you want.'

'That is well said,' said Odd, 'but it seems to me I may get a ship next summer and have no need to be your passenger.'

'You're not coming on this voyage,' said Gudmund, and with that they parted.

CHAPTER FOUR

Now Odd accepted his father's invitation to stay, and Grim sat him next to him, with Asmund on Odd's other side, and Grim made every hospitality available. But Gudmund and Sigurd lay anchored off the island half a month, and they waited for a fair wind.

One night Gudmund was restless in his sleep, and the men wondered if they should wake him. Sigurd said that he should dream his dream. Then Gudmund woke. 'What have you dreamed?' Sigurd said. 'I dreamed,' said Gudmund, 'that I thought I lay beside the island, but I saw that a polar bear lay in a ring around it, and its tail met with the head of the beast just above the ships, but it was the cruellest bear that I have ever seen, because its hair all stood on end, and it seemed to me then that it would throw itself at our ships and sink them both, when I awoke. Now you interpret the dream,' he said. 'I think,' said Sigurd, 'that there is little need to interpret it, because when you thought you saw this cruel bear with all its hairs turned forward, and you thought that it would sink the ship, I see clearly that it is the fetch of Odd, our kinsman, and he is angry with us. And this is why you thought the bear fierce towards us. This I can tell you that we will never get a fair wind to sail with us, unless he comes with us two.'

'He will now not join us even if we ask him,' said Gudmund. 'What shall we do, then?' Sigurd said. 'This I advise,' said Gudmund, 'that we go ashore, and invite him to come with us two.'

'What shall we do if he does not want to go?' said Sigurd. 'We shall give him one of our ships if he does not,' said Gudmund. They went ashore and found Odd and invited him to come with them. He said he would certainly not go. 'We will give you one of our ships, if you come with us,' said Gudmund. 'Then I shall go,' said Odd, 'and I am ready.'

Then Grim followed them to the ship. 'Here are some treasures that I shall give you, kinsman Odd,' said Grim. 'They are three arrows, and together they have a name, and are called Gusir's Gifts.' He then gave the arrows to Odd. He examined them and said: 'These are the greatest of treasures.' They were gold feathered, and they flew of their own accord, and back again, and there was never any need of looking for them. 'Ketil Trout took these arrows from Gusir, king of the Lapps. They bite all that they are told to, because they are dwarfs' work.'

'I have received no gifts,' said Odd, 'that I think equally fair,' and he thanked his father, and they parted in friendship, and Odd clambered aboard the ship and said that they should sail away from the island, and they unfurled the sails on Odd's ship, and so did they on the other.

Now they got a good wind and they sailed north to Finnmark, where the wind dropped, and they made for a harbour and stayed there that night, and there was a number of Lappish huts up from the shore. In the morning the crew went ashore from Gudmund's ship and raided each hut and plundered the Lapp women. They were angry at this treatment and yelled a lot. The crew on Odd's ship talked with Odd about going ashore, but he would not allow it. Gudmund came back to the ship that evening. Odd said, 'You went ashore?'

'That I did,' he said, 'and I had marvellous entertainment making the Lapp women shriek. Will you go with me tomorrow?'

'I will not,' said Odd.

When they had stayed for three nights, they got a fair wind, and there is nothing said of them until they got to Bjarmaland. They brought their ships to the river called the Dvina. Islands are numerous in that river. They cast anchor off a headland that jutted away from the mainland. Ashore they saw that many men had come out of the forest and gathered all in one place. Odd said, 'What do you think those people doing ashore, Gudmund?'

'I do not know,' he said, 'but what do you think, kinsman Odd?'

'I think,' he said, 'that this must be a great sacrifice or a funeral ale. Now you guard the ships, Gudmund, but Asmund and I will go ashore.' When they came to the forest, they saw a large building. Night was falling. They went to the door and took a look and saw many things. People were sitting on both benches. They saw that by the door was a vat. It was so well lit that there was no shadow, except behind the vat. It sounded as if the people within were happy. 'Do you know anything of their tongue?' said Odd. 'Not any more than birds' chirruping,' said Asmund. 'Or do you think you understand any of it?'

'No more than you,' said Odd. 'But do you see that one man serving drinks to both benches? I have a suspicion that he knows how to speak the Norse tongue. Now I will go in,' said Odd, 'and take up position where I think it is most hopeful, but you must await me here for a while.'

He then went in and took up a place near the entrance, and waited until the servant walked past. Then the servant found himself grabbed by Odd's hands and Odd lifted him over his head, but he shouted and told the Bjarmians that trolls had taken him. Then they sprang up and made for him on one side, but Odd fought them off with the servant. And it ended up that Odd and Asmund took the servant outside, and they did not feel brave enough to come out after them.

They came down to the ships with the servant, and Odd sat him on the seat with him and questioned him, but he held his peace. 'There is no need for that,' said Odd, 'because I know that you know how to speak the Norse tongue.' Then the servant said, 'What do you want to ask me?' Odd said, 'How long have you been here?'

'A few years,' he said. 'What do you think of it?' said Odd. 'I have never been,' said the servant, 'in a worse place than this.'

'What would you say,' said Odd, 'we could do that the Bjarmians would hate worst?'

'That's a good question,' he said. 'A mound stands on the riverbanks. It is made of two parts, silver and earth. Silver is placed there for each person who goes from the world, and so, when he came into the world, as much earth. The Bjarmians will think it the worst thing you can do if you go to the mound and bear away the silver.'

Odd called to Gudmund and Sigurd, and said. 'Your crew shall go to the mound following the servant's directions.' Then they prepared to go ashore, but Odd remained behind to guard the ships. The servant stayed with him.

CHAPTER FIVE

Then they went on till they came to the mound, and they gathered bags of treasure, because there was much silver. When they were ready, they went to the ships. Odd asked how it had gone, and they were cheerful and said there was no lack of loot. 'Now you shall,' said Odd, 'take the servant and watch him closely, because his eyes keep turning to the land as if he thought it not so bad with the Bjarmians as he let us think.' Odd went to the mound, but Gudmund and Sigurd guarded the ships. They sat and sifted the earth for silver, and the servant sat in between them, but then they saw him run up into the country, and they saw him no more.

It is said of Odd that he came to the mound. Odd said: 'Now we will gather bags ourselves, each after his own strength, so that our trip is not wasted.' It was dawn when they came away from the mound. They went until the sun had risen. Odd then halted. 'Why have you stopped?' said Asmund. 'I see a large crowd coming down from the forest,' said Odd. 'What shall we do now?' said Asmund. Then they all saw the crowd. 'This this does not look very good,' said Odd, 'for my quiver is back in the ship. Now I will go off into the forest and cut myself a club with this axe that I have in my hand, but you must go on to the headland that juts out into the river.' And so they did. When he came back, he had a big club in his hand. 'What do you think,' said Asmund, 'caused this crowd?'

'I think,' said Odd, 'that the servant escaped Gudmund and he has carried a warning of us to the Bjarmians, because I think that he thought being here was not as bad as he said. Now we must spread out in an array across the headland.'

Then the crowd hurried towards them, and Odd recognised the servant in the forefront. Odd called to him and said, 'Why did you lead us astray?' The servant said, 'I wished to learn what you liked best.'

'Where did you go?' said Odd. 'Inland,' he said, 'to tell the Bjarmians about you.'

'How do they like this business?' said Odd. 'I spoke up for you so well,' he said, 'that they will now do business with you.'

'That we will do gladly,' said Odd, 'when we get on board our ships.'

'It seems the Bjarmians think the least they could do is complete the business now.'

'What shall we trade?' said Odd. 'They want to

trade weapons and give you silver for iron.' 'We do not buy it,' said Odd. 'Then let us fight,' said the servant. 'It's up to you,' said Odd.

Then Odd told his band that they should throw into the river any corpses that fell from the enemy troop, - 'because they will immediately use their magic against us, if they reach of any of those who are dead.' After that the fight began, and Odd went through the ranks, wherever he came to them, and cut down the Bjarmians as if they were saplings, and it was both a hard fight and long. But in the end the Permians fled and Odd chased the fugitives and then turned back and examined his troop, and few had fallen, but the majority of the slain were people of the land. 'Now we can do business,' said Odd. 'Let us now collect silver weapons in heaps.' And so they did, and then went to their ships. When they got there, the ships were all gone. Then Odd seemed short of friends. 'What shall we now do?' said Asmund. 'There are two ways to see it,' said Odd. 'Either they have taken the ships round the other side of the islands, or they have betrayed us worse than we expected.'

'That cannot be,' said Asmund. 'I will try to find out,' said Odd.

He went to the wood and kindled a fire up in a big tree. It caught light so that the flame stood at ear height. Then they saw that ships were coming to land. There was a joyful meeting between the kinsmen, and they sailed away with the loot, and nothing is said of their journey until they came to Finnmark and into that same harbour as they had been earlier.

When night began, they woke to hear a great crash up in the air, like they had never heard before. Odd asked Sigurd and Gudmund if they had heard tell of this before anywhere. And when they were discussing these things, there was another crash, and that noise was not less than the first. Then came a third, and it was the greatest. 'What do you think, Odd,' said Gudmund, 'causes this?' Odd said: 'I have heard tell that two winds will blow at the same time in the air and clash and from their collision will come a big crash. Now we should expect bad weather to come.'

And they built a bulwark across their ships and prepared other things, after Odd's instructions, and it was all done, they had made their arrangements, when weather struck so evil that it drove them away from land, and they ran out of control and had to keep bailing. So the weather became so bad that they thought that their vessels would founder under them. Then Gudmund called from his ship to Odd and said: 'What should be done now?'

'One thing should be done now,' said Odd. 'What is that?' said Gudmund. 'Take all Lappish plunder and throw it overboard,' said Odd. 'What will that achieve?' said Gudmund. 'Let them decide that for themselves,' said Odd. It was done, the Lappish plunder was all broken up. Then they saw that it was driven along one side of the ship, and back the other, so that it came up into one mass, and then it was driven rapidly against the wind, so that it was soon out of sight. Soon after this they saw land, but the wind kept up and drove them to ashore, and they were then most exhausted except Odd and his kin and Asmund.

They reached the land now. It is not told how long they had been at sea. They unloaded their ships. Odd then advised that they drag their ships up and build strong defences. Then they set about it, and built themselves a hut. And when they had finished this, they explored the land. Odd thought that it must be an island. They saw that there was no lack of animals, and they shot them, as they needed food.

It happened one day when Odd had gone to the forest, he saw a huge bear. He shot at it and did not miss, and when the animal was dead, he flayed off the whole skin. Then he put a spike in its mouth and right through it. He let it stand mid-path, and facing towards the mainland. Odd had a happy time on the island.

But one evening, they were out when they saw a number of people on the mainland, and that crowd gathered on the headland, people both big and small. 'What do you think, kinsman Odd,' said Gudmund, 'that this crowd is?'

'I don't know,' said Odd, 'but I will try to go ashore and listen to what they are talking about.'

Odd asked Asmund to go with him. They went to the seaside, and stepped into the boat and rowed to the headland and put up oars and listened to the people talk. Now one who was a chief began to say, 'As you know, a few children have come to the island which we own, and done us great damage, and I come here to propose that we kill these squatters on our property. I have a bracelet on my arm. I will give it to those who will work their death.' A woman came forward to the assembly and said, 'We are fond of gewgaws, us women, so give me the ring.'

'Yes,' said the giant, 'you will do it well, the job which you carry out.'

Now to return to Odd, they went back home, and told them what had happened, what they had heard. But sooner than expected they saw that woman wading across the sound from the mainland to the island. She wore a leather robe, and was so large in size and evil-looking that they thought they had never seen such a creature. She went to the ships and took the two prows and shook them so that they thought the ships would all be broken. She walked up the path, but Odd put himself behind the bear. He had already put glowing embers in the mouth of the beast. He now took an arrow and shot it right through the beast. She saw the arrow that flew at her, and stopped it with the palm of her hand, and it bit no more than if it had hit stone. Then Odd took Gusir's Gifts and shot one like he had the first. She put up her other hand, and it went through it and into her eye and out the back of her head. She still came in their direction. Odd shot the third arrow. Then she put up her other hand and spat in it before, and it went as it had before, into her eye and out the back of the head. She now turned around and went back to the mainland and told them it had not gone smoothly. They stayed peacefully on the island for a while.

CHAPTER SIX

One evening, when they were there present outside their hut, they saw that a group had gathered on the headland as they had before. Odd and Asmund rowed to land and rested their oars. Then the chief spoke up on the headland. 'It is a great surprise,' he said, 'that we cannot kill these children. I sent there the noblest woman, but they have a creature that blows arrows and fire out of its nostrils and mouth, and now it follows that I am so sleepy that I must go home.' And so did Asmund and Odd.

Yet a third evening, they saw the same thing happen on the main land, and Odd and Asmund rowed there and listened. The same man began to speak up on the headland. 'It is as you know, that we have condemned these children, and nothing has come about, but now a vision is given to me.'

'What do you see now happening?' asked his comrades. 'What I see,' he said, 'is that here are two children arrived by boat, and they listen to what we say, and I will send them a gift.'

'Now we must be getting away quickly,' said

Odd. And immediately a stone flew from the headland and came down where their boat had been, and then they rowed back. Then the chief said, 'This is a great wonder! Their boat is still whole and so are they. I will throw another stone, and a third, but if they miss each time then I will leave them alone.' So great was the third stone that Odd's boat was flooded. Then they rowed away from the shore, and the giant began to speak: 'They are still safe and so is their boat, but now I am so sleepy that I cannot stay awake.' And then the giants went home. Odd said, 'Now it will make sense to pull the boat ashore.'

'What do you want do now?' said Asmund. 'Now I must know where this group lives.'

They went ashore and came to a cave, and a fire burned inside. They took up position and saw that trolls sat on both benches. An ogre sat on the throne. He was both big and evil-looking. He had long black hair like whalebone. He had a snotty nose and wicked eyes. His woman sat next to him. To describe one is to describe the other. Then the chief said, 'Now a vision is given to me, and I see the island, but now I know who they are who are there. They are kinsmen, the sons of Grim Hairycheek, Odd and Gudmund. I see that the Lapps have sent them here, and they believe that we shall kill them, but we cannot bring about that outcome, because I see that Odd is fated to live much longer than others. Now I will give them a wind to get away as fair as that the Lapps gave them to come here.' Odd said between his teeth: 'Of all men and trolls you give the worst gifts.'

'This I see, too, that Odd has the arrows called Gusir's Gifts, and so I will give him a name and call him Arrow-Odd.' Odd then took one of Gusir's Gifts and put it to the string, and intended to pay him back for his fair wind. When he heard the whine of the arrow that was upon him, he dodged it and collided with the rock, and the arrow came under one armpit of the woman and out the other, but she ran up and flew at the giant and scratched him. The trolls jumped up from both benches, and some helped him, but others his woman. Odd shot the second of Gusir's Gifts into the giant's eye and after that went to the ships, and the brothers were jubilant. 'How far did you go, Odd?' said Gudmund. Odd then recited a verse:

'I sought my goal

With Gusir's Gifts

Between the crags

And burning fire.

An ogre I hit

In the eye,

But in the ribs

His rock-lady.'

'We expected,' said Gudmund, 'that you would achieve much, seeing as you were so long away, or did something else happen during your journey?'

'A name was given to me,' said Odd and recited:

'I got my nickname,

That I have wished for,

Down from the crags

Ogres called it,

They said Arrow-

Odd they would give

A fine wind

To cross the waves.'

Wind was promised us to sail away from here, and I am told that the breeze will not be worse than that the Lapps gave us when we came here.'

They now readied themselves for the journey with as fine a show as before, and then went, and when they got some way from land the same gale as before struck them, so it swept them out to the sea, and often they had to bail, and they had no relief from the weather until they came to the same harbour as before, from which they had been driven, and then all the huts were derelict, and when they got a good wind they sailed to Hrafnista, arriving late in the winter. Grim was happy and invited them home with all his followers, and they accepted this offer. They put all their belongings into the hands of Grim and stayed with him for the winter.

CHAPTER SEVEN

Odd was so famous for this that no one thinks any other such thing has been achieved from Norway. There was great joy in the winter and much drinking. When spring came, Odd asked his kinsmen what they wished to do next. 'You can decide for us,' they said. 'Then I will go on Viking raids,' said Odd. He then told Grim that he wanted four ships to be readied to sail from the land. When Grim knew that, he took charge and told Odd when they were prepared. 'Now I want,' said Odd, 'you to direct us to some Viking you think worthy of us.' Grim said, 'Halfdan is the name of a Viking. He anchors in the east, off Elfar Skerries and has thirty ships.'

When they were ready, they sailed south round Norway, and when they came to the Elfar Skerries they found anchorage for their ships, but Halfdan was not far off. And when they had pitched their tents Odd went off with a few men to where the Vikings were moored. Odd saw a huge dragonship in the fleet. He called out to the ship and asked who the commander was. They lifted up the awnings, 'Halfdan is the name of this fleet's leader, but who asks?'

'He is called Odd.'

'Are the Odd who travelled to Bjarmaland?'

'I have been there,' said Odd. 'What is your errand here?' Halfdan said. 'I want to know which one of us is the greater man,' said Odd. 'How many ships have you?' Halfdan said. 'We have three vessels,' said Odd, 'all big ones with a hundred and twenty men aboard each, and we will be here tomorrow to meet with you.'

'We will sleep soundly despite that,' said Halfdan. Odd rowed away and came back to his people and told them what had happened. 'Now we will have a job,' said Odd, 'but I have now decided what we will do. We'll carry our cargo to land, put it ashore to make our ships lighter, but we will cut down some trees and put on each ship the largest and most leafy,' and so they did. And when they were ready, Odd said: 'I want you, Gudmund and Sigurd, to board the dragonship from the other side.' And so they did, and now quietly they rowed towards the ships which were anchored down the inlet. Odd rowed out to the dragonship, and when they were on both flanks, the vikings were taken by surprise, because the attackers swung trees against the dragonship with a man on every branch, and beat at the vikings through the tent awnings, and Odd and Asmund fought so fiercely that they had soon cleared the dragon up as far as the quarterdeck before Halfdan got to his feet, and they slew him there on the quarterdeck, and then Odd gave them two choices, if either they wanted to keep up the fight or give up, but they took the easier option and surrendered to Odd. He picked out all the men that he thought toughest. Odd took the dragonship into his possession and a second ship, but all other ships he gave to the Vikings. He took all the treasure himself. He gave the dragonship a name and called it Halfdan's Bequest.

They sailed home to Hrafnista having achieved a great victory, and stayed there over winter. But when spring came, Odd prepared to journey from the land. When they were ready, Odd asked his father, 'Where can we find a raider who is truly exceptional?' Grim said, 'Soti is the name of a Viking, and I will tell you how to get to him. He lies south of Skid. He has thirty ships and men.'

CHAPTER EIGHT

The kinsmen now moored in five ships south off Skida and sailed away from Hrafnista. But as the summer wore on Soti heard about Odd's movements and went to meet him and sailed day and night so that they might encounter each other. Then Soti ran into contrary winds, and he said, 'Let us lay our ships one alongside the other in a line, and I will put my boat in the middle, because I have heard that Odd is a daring man, and I think that he will sail his ships straight for us. But when they come and have reefed their sails, we will encircle their ships and let not one mother's son escape.'

Now to speak of the plans of Odd. 'I know what he and his men plan,' he said, 'They believe that we will sail straight at their vessels.'

'Will that not be rather unwise?' said Gudmund. 'Do not disappoint Soti,' said Odd, 'but we should take countermeasures. I think,' he said, 'I'll sail first in my dragonship to where Soti is. We'll clear the whole deck back to the mast.' And so they did, and the dragonship Halfdan's Bequest went fast. The ship was all covered with iron right round the prow, so it went with its keel just touching bottom. 'I intend to sail the dragonship straight for Soti,' said Odd, 'but you will sail in my wake. And I think that the ropes between their vessels will break.'

Odd sailed that dragonship as fast as it could go, but Soti learnt of his coming no earlier before he sailed straight up to him up and cut apart the links between the ships, and Odd and Asmund ran past the mast clad for war. They surprised him, rushed aboard the ship, and then they cleared the dragonship and killed him before Gudmund came to join them. Then Odd gave the Vikings the option whether they wanted to take peace from him or keep up the fight, but they decided on peace with Odd. Odd took the dragonship, but gave the other ships to the rest.

Then they sailed home to Hrafnista with great wealth, and Grim was happy to see them, and they stayed there over the winter in great respect. But when spring came, Odd readied the ships to sail, and he was now very choosy about the troop he picked to go along with him. Odd gave Gudmund and Sigurd the dragonship Soti's Bequest. He had the whole of the dragonship Halfdan's Bequest painted, and gilded both dragon heads and the weather vane. When the journey was prepared, Odd went to Grim, his father, and said, 'Now tell me where the best raider you know of is.'

'It is clear,' said Grim, 'that you are not satisfied with being great men, since it seems to you that no one could withstand you, but now I refer you to the best two Vikings I know of, and the best in everything. One is Hjalmar the Brave, and the other is called Thord Prow-Gleam.'

'Where are they,' said Odd, 'and how many ships do they have?'

'They have fifteen ships,' said Grim, 'and a hundred men aboard each.'

'Where is their homeland?' said Odd. 'Hlodver is the name of the King of Sweden. They stay with him in the winter, but stay aboard their warships in the summer.' And when they were ready, they went, and Grim went with them to the ships, and the father and son parted with much affection.

CHAPTER NINE

It is said of Odd that they sailed out from Hrafnista when they got wind, and nothing is told of their journey until they came to Sweden, at a place where one headland jutted out to sea from the mainland. They raised the awnings of their ships. Odd went ashore to see what was about, but there on the other side under the headland were fifteen ships and a camp on the land. He sees that there were games being played outside the tents. The leaders of these ships were Hjalmar and Thord.

Odd walked back to his ships, and told them the news. Gudmund asked what they should do. 'Now we will split our men in halves,' said Odd. 'You shall bring your ships around the headland and yell a war cry at the men on the shore, and I will walk overland with my half of the troop up into the forest, and we shall shout another battle cry at them, and it may be,' said he, 'that this will shake them. Come to think of it, they might flee into the woods and we won't need to do anything more.'

But it is said of Hjalmar and his men that when

they heard the battle cry of Gudmund that they didn't heed it, but when they heard another battle cry from the land, they stood still a while. And when the time of the war-cry was past, they played as before. Now both groups turned back from the headland, and Odd and Gudmund met. 'I don't know,' said Odd, 'that these people that we have met here are so easily frightened.'

'What will you now do?' said Gudmund. 'Quickly now is my advice,' said Odd, 'We should not sneak up on these men. Here we shall lie tonight beside the headland and wait here for tomorrow.' Then they went ashore with their troop up to meet Hjalmar, but when his men saw the Vikings ashore, then they armoured themselves to meet them. Hjalmar asked, when they met, who led the troop. Odd answered: 'There are more chiefs than one.'

'What is your name?' said Hjalmar. 'My name is Odd, son of Grim Hairycheek out of Hrafnista.'

'Are you the Odd that went to Bjarmaland recently? What is your errand here?'

'I want to know,' said Odd, 'who is the greater man of us.'

'How many ships do you have?' said Hjalmar. 'I have five ships,' said Odd, 'and how many troops have you?'

'We have fifteen ships,' said Hjalmar. 'It is heavy odds,' said Odd. 'Ten of my ships' crews shall sit back,' said Hjalmar, 'and we'll fight it out man to man.'

Then both sides prepared for battle and the troops lined up and fought while day lasted. In the evening the peace shield was held up, and Hjalmar asked Odd how he thought the day had gone. But he was very pleased. 'Do you want to continue the game?' said Hjalmar. 'I will not consider any other option,' said Odd, 'for that I have met no better boys or hardier men, and we will continue the fight in daylight.' And everyone did as Odd suggested, and they bound their wounds and returned to camp for the evening. But the morning after both sides drew up their troops for battle and fought all that day. And as the day wore on, they drew up a truce. Then Odd asked what Hjalmar thought of the battle that day. But he was very pleased. 'Do you want,' said Hjalmar, 'to have this game on a third day?'

'In this case, it would settle things between us,' said Odd. Then Thord said, 'Is there plenty of treasure and money in your ships?'

'Far from it,' said Odd, 'we have got no plunder this summer.'

'I think,' said Thord, 'that never have such foolish men met, because we fight for nothing, only pride and ambition.'

'What do you suggest we do?' said Odd. 'Do you not think it good advice,' said Thord, 'that we combine our efforts?'

'It pleases me well,' said Odd, 'but I am not sure what Hjalmar would think.'

'I want only the Viking laws,' said Hjalmar, 'which I have always had.'

'This I will know,' said Odd, 'when I hear them, how agreeable to me they are.'

Then Hjalmar: 'This is the first rule, that I will not eat raw meat, nor my troop, because it is many people's custom to squeeze flesh in cloth and call it cooked, but it seems to me that it's a custom more fit for wolves than humans. I will not rob merchants or farmers more than now and then to cover my immediate needs. I never rob women, even if we find them in the land alone with a lot of possessions, and no woman's to be taken to the ship to be raped, and if it may be that she is taken unwillingly, then he who does will lose his life whether he is rich or poor.' [2]

'Your laws seem good to me,' said Odd, 'and they will not stand in the way of our comradeship.' And then they joined forces, and it is said that now they had such a great troop that they had as many as Hjalmar had before they met.

CHAPTER TEN

After that Odd asked where they could expect to get loot. But Hjalmar said: 'On Zealand I know are five berserks, hardier than other men I have heard of, one called Brand, another Agnar, the third Asmund, fourth Ingjald, and fifth Alf. They are all brothers and have six vessels, all large. What do you say now, Odd, we do?'

'I want to sail,' said Odd, 'to where the berserk are.' They came to Zealand with their fifteen ships and heard the news that berserks were gone ashore to meet their mistresses. Then Odd went ashore alone to meet them. And when they met, a battle began, and it ended up that he killed them all, but was not wounded. When Odd went ashore, Asmund missed him and spoke to Hjalmar, 'Yes,' he said, 'There is no doubt that Odd has gone ashore, so we should not be idle meanwhile.' Hjalmar sailed with six ships to where the other Vikings were, and began a battle, and just as Odd came down from the land Hjalmar had taken the ship. And now they told each other their news, and both had amassed wealth and honours.

Now Hjalmar invited Odd to come with him to

Sweden, and Odd accepted. But the Halogalanders, Gudmund and Sigurd, went north to Hrafnista with their troops, agreeing to meet again at the Gautelf. When Hjalmar and the rest reached Sweden, King Hlodver welcomed them with open arms, and they stayed there for the winter, and much honour was done to Odd, because the king thought he had no match. Odd had been there only a little while before the king gave him five farms. The king had an only daughter, named Ingibjorg. She was very attractive and skilled in womanly arts. Odd asked Hjalmar why he did not ask for Ingibjorg's hand, - 'because I see that both your hearts beat as one.'

'I have asked her,' he said, 'but the king will not give his daughter to anyone who doesn't have a king's rank.'

'Then we shall gather the army next summer,' said Odd, 'and give the king two choices, fight us and or give you his daughter.'

'I'm not sure about that,' said Hjalmar, 'because I have long had sanctuary here.' They stayed there quietly for the winter. But in the spring they went raiding when they were ready.

CHAPTER ELEVEN

Now nothing is told of their journey until they met at the Gautelf, and discussed where they should sail that summer. Odd said most of all he was for going west over the sea. Then they had twenty vessels and Odd skippered the dragonship Halfdan's Bequest. They came to Scotland, and made raids there, harrying and burning everywhere where they went, and there was no stopping them until they laid everywhere under tribute. From there they went to the Orkneys, and they put them under them and stayed there for the winter. But in the spring they went to Ireland and raided both along the sea and inland. Odd went nowhere without Asmund with him. But children and women and men fled away into the woods and forests, hiding their possessions and themselves.

There was a day when Odd and Asmund were together some way up-country. Odd had his quiver on his back, and a bow in his hand, and they wanted to see if they could find anyone. Now before Odd suspected, a bowstring hummed and an arrow flew from the wood and it hit Asmund, and he fell and died quickly. This seemed to Odd the worst news he had suffered in his lifetime. He went ashore, but left Asmund there, and Odd was in so evil a mind, he intended nothing else but give the Irish all the hurt he could, whatever came to mind. He came at once to a clearing where a large number of women and men stood. He saw a man in a very expensive tunic, and with a bow in his hand, but the arrows were in the ground before him. Odd was sure that he would find his revenge where the man was. He took out an arrow, one of Gusir's Gifts, and laid it to the bowstring, and aimed at this man. It struck him in the middle, and then he fell down dead. Now he shot at the others, so that he killed three more. And now the people fled into the forests. Odd was so evil in heart to the Irish that he meant to do them all that harm he was able. He now went up a great forest path. He tore up every shrub by the roots that was in his way. He pulled up one shrub, which was less firmly rooted than the others. Then he saw a door and pulled it up and went down into the ground. There he found four women in an earth-house[3], and one was far more attractive than the others. He seized her hand and tried to pull her out of the house. She spoke then and said: 'Let me loose, Odd,' she said.

'What troll are you,' he said, 'to know I am named Odd and not anything else?'

'I knew,' she said, 'when you came here, who

you were, and I know that Hjalmar is with you, and I know to tell him if I am taken unwillingly to the ships.'

'Nevertheless, you'll come,' said Odd. Now the women took hold of her and wanted to keep her there, but she ordered them stop. 'I will bargain with you,' she said, 'you should let me go in peace, for I have no lack of treasure.'

'Far from it that I want your treasure,' said Odd, 'for I don't lack gold or silver.'

'Then I will make you a shirt,' she said. 'It is still the case,' said Odd, 'that I have enough of shirts and shirt-making.'

'You will never have,' she said, 'such a shirt as that I will make, because it shall be sewn with gold, and made out of silk. I will give the shirt qualities so you will not have had such great virtues before.'

'Let me hear them,' said Odd. 'You shall never be cold in it, neither by sea nor on land. You shall not be tired when swimming, and nor will fire hurt you, and never shall hunger grip you, and iron shall not bite you, and it will ward you from all things except one.'

'What's that?' said Odd. 'Iron will bite you,' she said, 'if you retreat, even if you're in the shirt.'

'I've better things to do in battle than to flee,' said Odd, 'and by when shall it be made?'

'By next summer,' she said, 'at the same time of day as now, and with the sun in the south. Then we will meet here in this same clearing.'

'What do you think,' said Odd, 'I will do to you Irish then, if you do not fulfil this, as I have much to pay back for what they did to Asmund?'

'Do you think you still have not avenged him,' she said, 'when you have killed my father and my three brothers?'

'It does not seem to me that I have avenged him at all,' said Odd. They settled their deal and went their ways.

Odd went to where Asmund was, took him up now and laid him on his back and so went down to the sea. Hjalmar had come ashore with all his men, and was looking for Odd. They met near the ship, and Hjalmar asked what had happened, and Odd told him. 'Did you avenge him?' said Hjalmar. Poetry sprang to Odd's lips:

'I ran down that wide

Wagon trail road,

To the fierce arrows

I turned my face.

To have Asmund back

By my side

I would give

All my gold.'

'What shall we do now?' said Hjalmar. 'You'll now want to plunder here, and do evil everywhere.'

'Far from it,' said Odd, 'because I want now to be off quickly.' The Vikings were very surprised by this. But Hjalmar said it should be as Odd wished. They raised a howe over Asmund. The Vikings were angry about this, and they grumbled about Odd behind his back. But he acted as though he did not know it.

They sailed west until they came to Hlesey. An earl, who is not named, was there and he had thirty ships. They met in battle, and there was a fierce fight. Odd then cleared himself of the coward's name that the Vikings gave him in Ireland. Odd and Hjalmar won the victory in this battle. From there, they sailed to Denmark where they heard the news that a troop had been mustered against them to avenge the five berserks who they had defeated before they went west to Ireland. Two earls led the troop, and it ended so when they met they killed them both, and took tribute from the land.

CHAPTER TWELVE

Now they divided their forces, and Gudmund and Sigurd sailed north to Hrafnista, and they settled there quietly and decided to give up raiding. But Odd stayed in Denmark for the winter, while Hjalmar went to Sweden with his followers, and they agreed to meet east in Skane in the spring, and both stayed quietly at home over the winter. In the spring, Hjalmar and Thord Prowgleam sailed from the east at the time agreed for them to meet. When they met, Hjalmar asked where Odd wanted to go that the summer. But he said that he wanted to go to Ireland. 'You didn't want to plunder there last summer,' said Hjalmar. 'However it might have then,' he said, 'I shall now go there in the summer.'

Now they sailed from the land, and they had a good wind until that they came to Ireland. Odd said: 'Let us camp here, but I will go up-country alone.'

'I will come with you,' said Hjalmar. 'I will go

alone,' said Odd, 'because I am seeing here some women in the woods.' Odd went until he came to that same clearing where Olvor had agreed to meet him, and she had not come. He was already filled with great anger for the Irishmen and right away resolved to harry the land. But after he had gone thus for a while, he heard some carts coming towards him. He found it was Olvor, and she greeted him first, 'Now I hope you won't be angry with me, though I am later than I said.'

'Is the shirt done?' said Odd.

'I do not doubt it,' she said, 'and now you shall sit down with me, and I will see how well the shirt fits you.' And so he did, took it and unfolded it and put it on, and it fitted perfectly in all respects.

'Do all the qualities go with the shirt,' said Odd, 'that you spoke of?'

'They do,' she said.

'How so,' said Odd. 'Did you make this treasure yourself?' Then poetry came to her lips:

'This shirt is sewn out of silk

From six lands:

An arm in Ireland,

The other with Lapps in the north,

Started by Saxon maidens,

But Sutherey women spun it,

Welsh wives wove it,

On the warp of Othjodan's mother.'

Then poetry came to Odd's lips:

'Not like the hauberk

Of blue rings

Ice cold about me

Upon my body,

When down my sides,

This silk shirt,

Gold embroidered,

Went close.'

'How do you find the shirt?' she said.

But he was well pleased. 'Now, choose your reward for the shirt,' said Odd.

'Here there has been little happiness,' she said, 'since my father was slain, and the land is running out of my control. Therefore I will choose the reward that you stay here three winters.'

'Then we must make another deal,' said Odd, 'and you can come with me and be my wife.'

'You must think me eager to get a husband,' she said, 'but I shall accept.' Then Odd looked around and saw nearby a group of warriors. He asked if this troop was sent to kill him. 'Far from it,' she said. 'These men shall accompany you down to your ships, and you will now leave with more honour than last summer.' He returned to his ship and these warriors with him, and they met Hjalmar at the tents.

Now Odd asked Hjalmar to stay with him for three winters, and so he agreed. Odd now married Olvor. But in the summer they stayed aboard their warships and killed the Vikings attacking there. And when they had sat there for such a time as was decided, they had wiped out all the vikings, both near and far in Ireland, some were killed, while some fled. By then Odd was so tired of being there that nothing could discourage him from leaving.

Olvor and Odd had a girl called Ragnhild. They argued about it because Odd wanted to take her with him, but Olvor refused this. They asked Hjalmar about it, and he said that the girl should grow up with her mother.

When they were ready, they sailed away and came to England. They heard that there lay a Viking named Skolli, and he had forty ships. And when they dropped anchor, Odd went off in a boat and wanted to have words with Skolli. But when they met, he asked Odd what errand he had in that country. 'I mean do battle with you,' said Odd. 'Why do you want to do me harm?' said Skolli. 'Nothing,' said Odd, 'but I will have your treasure and life because you are making war on the king who is ruler here.' His name was Edmund. 'Are you the Odd,' said Skolli, 'who went to Bjarmaland a long time ago?'

'This is the same man,' said Odd. 'I am not so vain,' said Skolli, 'that I'm going to think myself your equal. Now you must learn why I fight King Edmund.'

'Well that I may,' said Odd. 'The king killed my father here in the country, and many of my kin, and then he settled in the realm. But I have sometimes seized half of the country, and sometimes a third. Now I think you would get greater glory if you combined your troop with mine, and we kill King Edmund, and put the realm under us. I will seal this deal with witnesses.'

'Please,' said Odd, 'summon eight farmers off the land to swear oaths on your behalf.'

'So shall it be,' said Skolli. Now Odd went to their ships and found Hjalmar and told him that if it went as Skolli had said, they should fight alongside him. They now slept through the night. In the morning they went ashore with all their followers. Skolli had been busy that night, and he had come down from the land with the farmers, and they swore oaths of support. After that they joined their forces and went up-country and went to war, burning everything and destroying everything which they came to. But the people fled away and went to the king. However, in the south of the country they met, and the battle began between them, and they fought for three days. And it ended that King Edmund fell there. Odd laid the land under him and stayed there for the winter. In the spring Skolli offered to give him the land. Odd refused to accept, - 'but I can suggest you give it to Hjalmar.' But Hjalmar refused. 'In that case,' said Odd, 'we should give Skolli the land.' And he accepted it, and said that they could stay there at any time they wanted, whether it was winter or summer. They now equipped twenty ships to sail from the land, and nothing is told of their journey until they came south of Skida.

CHAPTER THIRTEEN

Two kings are mentioned. One was named Hlodver, the other Haki. They were there with thirty ships. When Odd and his men lay with their ships by the shore, ten ships came rowing at them. And when they met, no words were bandied, because at once a battle broke out between them. Odd had twenty ships. They attacked so hard that Odd had scarcely ever come to such a pass that he had been so sorely pressed. But in the end it worked out that they defeated the ten ships. Then Odd said, 'They were hardly the terrors they have been reported as.'

'Do you think that?' said Hjalmar. 'These were the scouts of the men who were sent out to meet us.' But they rested little time, then the twenty ships from offshore rowed towards them, and at once broke out a battle so hard and intense, that Odd had never met such great men, neither at sea, nor on land. And the fighting ended up with both kings dead and all with them. As it is told, Odd and Hjalmar had no greater force than they could sail away with in one boat, and they came to the islands that are called the Elfar Skerries. In the islands are creeks called Tronuvagar. They saw there were two ships, and with black awnings over them both. This was the beginning of the summer. 'Now I don't want them,' said Hjalmar, 'to notice us, for those vikings lie quiet under the awnings.'

'I cannot accept,' said Odd, 'that I have no words with men who I meet on my way.'

Now Odd called and asked who was in charge of the ships. A man lifted the hem of the awnings, and said, 'That man is called Ogmund.'

'Which Ogmund are you?' said Odd. 'Where have you been that you have not heard tell of Ogmund Eythjof's-Bane?' the shipman said. 'I have heard tell of you,' said Odd, 'and never have I seen such an evil-looking person as you.' It is said about this man that he was black of hair, and a tuft hung down over the face where the forelock should have been, but nothing was seen of his face except his teeth and eyes. He had eight men with him, much the same in looks. No iron bit them. They were more like giants than men in terms of stature and evil. Then Ogmund said, 'Who is the man finding fault with me so?'

'He's called Odd,' he said.

'Are you the Odd,' said Ogmund, 'that went to Bjarmaland a long time ago?'

'That is the man,' said Odd, 'who has come.'

'It is good,' said Ogmund, 'for I have sought you for most of my life.'

'What have you my mind?' said Odd. 'Where would you fight, at sea or on land?' Ogmund said. 'I will fight at sea,' said Odd. Then Ogmund and his men took down the awnings. Hjalmar and his crew made ready and loaded stones in his ship. And when they were ready on either side, they had some hard fighting, and lay their ships next to each other. They had a long and hard battle. And when it had gone on for a while, Ogmund raised a peace flag and asked Odd how he thought it went. He said that he thought it went ill. 'Why is that?' Ogmund said. 'Because I have always fought with men before, but now I should think I fight Hel,' said Odd. 'I hacked at your neck before, which I thought easy with the sword I hold, and it did not cut.' Ogmund answered: 'Each of us could say about the other, that he is more a troll than a man. I hacked at your neck, which I thought easy, and the sword I used has never wavered in the fight before, and it did not bite, and do you now wish that we fight anymore?' said Ogmund, 'or do you wish that we part, because I can tell you how the battle will: here will die the sworn brothers, Hjalmar and Thord, and your troop too. Then will all my warriors die, and only we two will remain standing. But if we fight it out, I will fall to you,' said Ogmund. 'On with the game then,' said

Odd, 'until all my troop is wiped out, and yours.' They thrust shields together a second time and fought until only three remained standing, Thord, Hjalmar and Odd. But Ogmund still stood, and eight with him. He spoke: 'Do you now, Odd, want to part, because I now call equal numbers of slain, because things will go as I told you, but you are meant to live much longer than others. You have a shirt that means you cannot be hurt.'

'It seems better to me,' said Odd, 'to part sooner than later as long as you put no name of coward on me.'

'Then we break off now,' Ogmund said, 'Because I call our numbers of slain equal.' Odd said he wanted to get away from the creeks, and they did so, and went to an island. Odd said that three things lay ahead: one was go to the forest and shoot animals, second, to guard the ship. 'I will light a fire,' said Hjalmar, 'and do the cooking.' Odd went to the forest, but Thord kept the ship. When they came back, Thord was gone. They went and looked for him. They found the boat in which he had been securely tied. They looked for Thord and found him in a rock crevice. He had sat there and died. 'This is an evil event,' said Odd, 'We have not had such a loss since Asmund died.' They now look for what caused his death, and found that a spear is under one arm, but the head came out the other. 'That villain Ogmund thought,' said Odd, 'that we weren't even. We shall put into the bays to search for them.' And so they did, but Ogmund had gone away. They sought him through all the skerries, forests, islands and headlands and did not find him, nor hear of him. They went back to Thord, and brought him to Sweden and raised a burial mound over him. Then they went home to Uppsala and told the king the news. The king received them with open arms, and they sat quietly, but when summer came again the king invited them to stay there - 'and I will give you both a ship and crew from the land, so that you may entertain yourselves.'

CHAPTER FOURTEEN

It is now told of Odd that they fitted out two ships and he had forty men on each ship. They sailed from the land. Then they were exposed to bad weather, and they came to an island called Samsey. There are bays there called Munarvag. They anchored their ships and raised the awnings. But during the day the gable head on Odd's boat had broken. When morning came, Odd and Hjalmar went ashore to chop down a tree. Hjalmar was accustomed to walk wearing all his armour which he had while fighting. Odd had left his quiver down at his ship, but he wore his shirt day and night. The whole of their troop was asleep. Vikings attacked them by surprise, and their leader was named Angantyr. [4] They were twelve in number, and were all brothers. By this time they had gone around the world and nowhere met resistance. Now they came to where the ships of Odd and Hjalmar were. They attacked the men aboard, and to make a long story short they killed every man on the ships. Then the brothers spoke and said thus: 'It is the case that Arngrim, our father, never said a bigger lie but when he told us these men were hard and mighty vikings, so that no one could stop them, but where we have gone no one has borne himself worse and shown less fight. Let's go home and kill that shit of a man as payback for his lies.'

'There is another question,' said some, 'either Odd and Hjalmar have been most over-praised, or else they have gone ashore, since the weather is good. Let us go ashore and look for them rather than go back untried.' Now the twelve brothers did so, and now came the berserk fit, and they went roaring. Then the berserk fit came upon Angantyr, but it had never happened to him before. Just then Odd and Hjalmar came down from the woods. Now Odd stopped and hesitated. Hjalmar asked what it was. Odd said, 'Something odd keeps happening to me. Sometimes I think that bulls or dogs are yelling, but sometimes it is like men somewhere screaming, and do you know whose nature it is to behave thus?'

'Yes,' said Hjalmar, 'I know the twelve brothers.'

'Do you know their names?' said Odd. Then a verse came to Hjalmar's lips:

'Hervard, Hjorvard,

Hrani, Angantyr,

Bild and Bui,

Barri and Toki,

Tind and Tyrfing,

Two Haddings,

East in Bolm

They were bairns,

Sons of Arngrim

And of Eyfura.

I learned that these men

Are malevolent

And most dishonourable

In their acts.

They are berserks,

Bringers of evil,

Our two ships they swept

Of our loyal sailors.'

Then Odd saw the berserks legging towards them, and poetry came to his lips:

'*I see men walking*

War-hungry

From Munarvag

In grey mailcoats.

Vile the fight

These men have fought.

Broken our ships

On the beach.'

Odd said: 'It is no good,' he said, 'because I left my quiver and bow when we left the ships, but I have this axe in my hand.' Odd then recited a verse:

'I felt fear

Once,

When they bellowed,

Leaving the longships

(And screaming

Ascended the island)

Inglorious,

Twelve men together.'

Odd then went back to the forest and cut a club, but Hjalmar waited for his return. When he came back, then the berserks came legging up to them. Whereupon Hjalmar said:

'Mighty are the warriors

Leaving the warships,

Twelve men together

Inglorious;

I think this evening

I will be Odin's guest,

Two sworn brothers,

But the twelve will live.'

Then Odd followed with:

'To your word will I

Provide an answer:

They will this evening

Be Odin's guests,

Twelve berserks,

We two shall live.'

Then a verse came to Angantyr's lips:

'It has gone

Hard for you

All your fellows.

Have fallen

And you must follow,

And feast in the hall.'

Then Odd said:

'There are come

Trudging together,

Inglorious,

Those twelve.

One by one, the

Battle waging

Is the hero's way,

Unless his heart fails.'

'Who are these people,' said Odd, 'that we meet here?'

'There is a man named Angantyr,' said the other, 'who is the leader. We are twelve brothers, the sons of Earl Arngrim and of Eyfura from east Flanders[5]. And who asks?' Angantyr said. 'This one is called Odd, son of Grim Hairy-cheek, the other is called Hjalmar the Brave.'

'A warm welcome,' said Angantyr, 'for we have sought you widely.'

'Did you go to our vessels?' said Odd. 'We went there,' said Angantyr, 'and we've taken everything for ourselves.'

'How do you feel now,' said Hjalmar, 'about our meeting?'

'I think,' said Angantyr, 'we should do what you said earlier, fight this one to one, and I want to fight you, Odd, because you have a shirt that means that iron shall not bite you, but I have a sword that is called Tyrfing and dwarves forged it and promised that could bite through anything, even iron or stone. We shall divide our troop into halves, and have seven in one group, and I and four men in the other. I am said to be equal to the two Haddings. Then there's one more against Tyrfing.' Then Hjalmar said, 'I will fight Angantyr, because I have armour which has kept me from acquiring wounds. It has fourfold rings.'

'It would be a bad idea,' said Odd, 'for we will do well if I fight with Angantyr, but it will be hopeless otherwise.'

'However it goes,' said Hjalmar, 'I shall prevail.' Then Angantyr: 'I want this,' said Angantyr, 'If anyone survives here, let no one rob the dead of weapons. I would have Tyrfing in the mound with me, if I die. And so Odd shall have his shirt and arrows, and Hjalmar his armour.' And so they agreed that they must raise a burial mound over the dead, if they live.

Now first approached the two Haddings, but Odd smote each with his club, and they did not need more. Then one came after the other to fight Odd, and so it ended up that he killed all who came against him. Now Odd took a rest. Then Hjalmar stood up and someone came against him in the contest. They closed their business when he fell. Then came a second, and a third and a fourth. Then came Angantyr, and they fought hard and long, and so it ended up that Angantyr fell before Hjalmar. Then Hjalmar went to a hillock and sat down and sank against it. Odd went to him and recited:

'What worries you, Hjalmar?

Your colour is wan.

Wasting your strength

Are multiple wounds;

Your helmet is hacked,

And the hauberk on your chest,

Now I deem you have seen

The end of your days.'

'And have proved that which I told you, that you would not listen to, if you fought with Angantyr.'

'That doesn't matter,' said Hjalmar, 'everyone has their time to die,' and he said this:

'I have sixteen wounds; my byrnie is split,

My sight is darkened, I cannot see.

Angantyr's blade entered my heart:

That sharp sword was steeped in poison.'

'Now I have had a loss,' said Odd, 'that will never be made good as long as I live, and it has now gone badly because of your obstinacy, and we would have got here a great victory, if I had had my way.'

'Now, settle down,' said Hjalmar, 'and I will compose a poem and send it home to Sweden with you.' He said this:

'They'll never hear,

The women back home

That I ever cringed

From sword cuts.

They'll not tease me

About me retreating,

The sly girls

At Sigtuna.

I sailed away from the songs of women,

Eagerly voyaging eastwards with Soti;

Travelling swiftly after joining a troop,

Left at last my friends in the hall.

I went from the white cloaked woman,

To Agnafit on the edge of the sea;

It is true what she told me there,

That I would never be near her again.

I abandoned her, young Ingibjorg,

Hastily determined,

The day of destiny.

She will soon mourn me,

Bitter in her mind

But never again

Shall we meet each other.

Carry there to display,

From my combat,

Helmet and mailcoat

To the royal hall.

Tears will drop

King's daughter,

When she sees broken

The byrnie on my breast.

Five were the farms I had for my own,

But never have I known joy of them;

Now I must lie with my life taken,

Wounded by the sword on Samsey.

Slip the red-gold ring from my hand,

And bear it to young Ingibjorg;

Her misery will remain in her thoughts,

For I'll never be seen in Uppsala again.

Well I remember sitting

With the women persuading

Me not to set out

From there.

Hjalmar will never

Know joy in the king's hall,

Fine company or ale.

Now I wish, too, that you bear my greetings to all our bench companions, and I will mention them by name:

We drank and talked

Many a day,

Alf and Atli,

Eyvind, Trani,

Gizur, Glama,

Gudvard, Starri,

Steinkel, Stikill,

Storolf, Vifil.

Hrafn and Helgi,

Hlodver, Igull

Stein and Kari,

Styr and Ali,

Ossur, Agnar,

Orm and Trandill,

Gylfi and Gauti,

Gjafarr and Raknarr.

Fjolmund, Fjalar,

Frosti and Beinir,

Tindall and Tyrfing,

Two Haddings,

Valbjorn, Vikar,

Audbjorn, Flosi,

Geirbrand, Goti,

Guttorm, Sneril.

Styr and Ari,

Stein and Kari,

Vott, Vesela,

Audbjorn, Hnefi.

We all shared a single bench

Sat at ease;

As a result I am

Reluctant to flee.

Svarfandi, Sigvaldi,

Saebjorn and Kol,

Thrain and Thiostolf,

Thorolf and Sval,

Hrapp and Hadding,

Hunfast, Knui,

Ottar, Egil,

Ingvar and all.

'Now I would ask you,' said Hjalmar of Odd, 'that you do not lay me in a mound beside such evil fiends as these berserk are, for I deem myself much better than they were.'

'That I will give you,' said Odd, 'as you ask, because now it seems to me that you are rapidly going.'

'Now, pull the ring from my hand,' said Hjalmar, 'and bring it to Ingibjorg, and tell her that I sent it to her on my dying day.' Now poetry came to Hjalmar's lips:

'The earls sit

All drinking

Ale heartily

In Uppsala.

Many warriors

Weaken at beer,

But alone with my wounds

On the island I suffer.

From the east the raven flies, abandons his bough,

After him the eagle flies as well:

I feed him with flesh for a final time,

Now he will guzzle my dripping gore.

And after that Hjalmar died. Odd dragged the berserks together in a heap and piled timber around them. It was not far from the sea. Here, he laid with them their weapons and clothes, and he robbed none of them. Then he covered them with turf and after that sand. Then he took Hjalmar and laid him on his back, and went down to the sea, and he set him down on the beach, but he went out to the ship, carried to the land every man who had fallen, and lay them in another mound, and it is said by those who have gone there since that you can still see signs today of what Odd did then.

CHAPTER FIFTEEN

After that Odd put Hjalmar aboard the ship and set out to sea. Then Odd used his magic, hoisted sail in calm weather and sailed back to Sweden with Hjalmar's corpse. He landed at a place he had chosen. He beached his ship, and put Hjalmar on his back and went to Uppsala with him and set him down in the entrance hall. He went into the hall and carried Hjalmar's armour in his hand and also his helmet and laid them down in the hall before the king and told him what had happened.

Then he went to where Ingibjorg was sitting on a chair. She was sewing a shirt for Hjalmar. 'Here is a ring,' said Odd, 'that Hjalmar sent you on his dying day and greets you with.' She took the ring and looked at it, but said nothing. She sank down then back against the chair posts and died. Odd then burst out laughing and said: 'It is not often that things have gone well recently, so I should be rejoicing. Now they shall enjoy each other dead, which they could not in life.' Odd took her up and carried her in his arms, and laid her in the arms of Hjalmar in the entrance hall, and sent men into the hall after the king and asked him to see how he had done this. After that the King welcomed him, and set Odd on the throne with him. But when he had taken a rest, the king told him that he wanted to hold a funeral ale for Hjalmar and Ingibjorg and raise a burial mound for them. So the king ordered everything to be done as Odd said. When the helmet and armour that Hjalmar had worn was displayed, it seemed he had been a great man worthy of his achievements and the spirit with which he had defended himself, and now they were lying both in one pile. So all the people came to see this remarkable work, for Odd had made it with great honour. Odd now sat quietly over winter with King Hlodver, but in the spring the king gave him men and ten ships, and then in the summer Odd went to look for Ogmund Eythjof's-Bane again but could not find him.

CHAPTER SIXTEEN

So it came to pass in the autumn that Odd came to Gautland. There he heard about a Viking named Saemund. He was told that he was harder to deal with than others. He had fifty five ships. Odd came to him with ten ships, and when they met there was a battle long and hard, with no lack of deeds. And it ended up that evening that all vessels belonging to Odd had been cleared and he was the last of his side standing. Odd jumped overboard when it was near dark. A man saw this. He snatched up a throwing spear, and hurled it after him. It caught in Odd's calves so that it hit the bone. It came to his mind, the way things were at present, he could be said to be on the run. He swam back to the ships, but the Vikings saw Odd and pulled him into the boat. Saemund told them to fix shackles to his feet, and bind his hands with a bow string. It was done as he told them.

Now Odd sat in fetters, and twelve men were told to watch over him, but Saemund had himself taken to the shore and set up camp. Odd said to those who had been told to watch over him, 'Do you wish that I entertain you, or do you wish to entertain me, since it's so dull work?'

'We reckon,' said he who led them, 'that you may not give much entertainment while you are in chains, and meant to be killed tomorrow.'

'I am not afraid of that,' said Odd. 'Everyone has their time to die.'

'Then we choose that you entertain us,' they said. He began to sing and did not stop until they were all asleep. Then Odd crawled to where an axe was lying on the bulkheads. He also managed to twist it so that the edge faced up. Then he turns his shoulders, and rubbed his hands against until he was free. He untied the fetters and got them off his feet. And when he was free, it seemed to him he had room to move. Now he went to where they slept, and prodded them with the axe handle and told them wake up, - 'because as you slept like fools, the prisoner has got free.' Then he killed them all, took his quiver and climbed into the boat and rowed ashore. Then he went to the woods and pulled the spearhead out his foot, and bound up his wound.

Now it is told of Saemund that he woke up in the tent, and sent men out to the ships where the guards were, and learnt that Odd was away and had killed all the guards, and they missed their friends and went to Saemund and told him what had happened, and now he searched everywhere in Gautland seeking Odd, but Odd was in a different place seeking Saemund.

It was early one morning that Odd came out from the wood. He saw Saemund's tents on the shore, but the ships out in the harbour. He turned back into the forest and cut a club, came down to the tent and felled it on top of Saemund and his men. He killed Saemund and then fourteen more. Then he gives them choices, those aboard, that they shall accept his guidance and make him their chief, and that they preferred. Odd now went home to Sweden and he had but a small troop, and he stayed there over the winter.

CHAPTER SEVENTEEN

Then Odd sent messengers north to Hrafnista and asked his kin to join him, so Gudmund and Sigurd would come from the north in the spring. They were glad and went to Odd. And when they met, there was a joyful meeting.

Afterwards, they set sail from the land in their ships and keep south hugging the cost, and the water was much shallower, and Odd had never been there before. They now plundered southern Gaul, Frankland and Halsingjaland. Here they wreaked havoc.

Nothing is told of their journey until they wrecked their ships on a certain shore. Here they went ashore with their troops. As they went inland, they saw a house before them. It was built in some way they had never seen before. Up they went to the house. It was made of stone and the door was open. Odd said, 'What do you think, Sigurd, is this house that we have here?'

'I do not know,' he said. 'But what do you think,

kinsman Odd?'

'I am not sure,' he said, 'but I expect that men live in the house and will come back here, and we shall not go in as things stand.' They settle down in a place outside the house, but after a while, they saw people hurrying to the house, and also they heard a noise which they had never heard before. 'I think,' said Odd, 'that these are very strange men in this country. We shall now wait here till they come from the house.' It went as Odd guessed, that the time drew near, and the men hurried from the house. One of the local people went where Odd sat, and said, 'Who are you?' Odd told him the truth, - 'and what country is this that we've come to?' The person said that this place was Aquitania. 'But what is this house where you have been standing for a while?'

'This we call either the minster or church.'

'But what kind of noise is it you have been making?'

'That we call the Mass,' said the local man. 'But what about you, are you an utter heathen?' Odd said, 'We do not have any faith, we believe in our might and main, but we don't believe in Odin, but what religion you have?' the man said: 'We believe in him that created heaven and earth, the sea, the sun and moon.' Odd said: 'He who has built all that must be great, that I can understand.'

Now Odd and his men were shown to lodgings. They were there several weeks and had some meetings with the locals. They asked them and Odd, if they would take the faith, and in the end Gudmund and Sigurd converted. They asked Odd if he would take the faith. He said he would offer them a deal, 'I will take your faith, but I will act the same as before. I will sacrifice neither to Thor nor Odin or other idols, but I am no mood to be in this place. Therefore I will wander from land to land, and be sometimes with pagans, sometimes with Christians.' In the end, however, Odd was baptized. They stayed there for a while.

One time Odd asked Sigurd and Gudmund if they would go away. They say: 'We have liked being here more than elsewhere.'

'Then here is a disagreement,' said Odd, 'I have been so bored here because nothing has happened.' He did not ask leave from his brothers, stealing away alone, but they stayed along with all their people.

And as he came away from the city, he saw a large group of people coming towards him. One man rode while the others walked. These people were all clad elegantly, and no one carried weapons. Odd stood by the street, but the people went past him, and did not speak to each other. Then Odd saw where four men ran. They all had long knives in their hands. They ran to the man who was riding, and cut off his head. Then they ran back past Odd the same way, and one had in his hand the head of the man who was killed. Odd thought he knew that they had done great evil. Now Odd ran after them and chased them, but they ran away to the forest, and went to ground in an earth-house there. Odd ran after them into the earth-house. Because they showed resistance, Odd attacked them. He gave them no relief until he had killed them all. Then he took their heads by the hair, and tied them together, then went out and carried their heads and the head that they had when they went there. Odd went back to the city. Then there were others come to church with the corpse of the man who was killed. Odd threw the heads into the minster and said: 'There is the head of the man who was killed, and I have avenged him.' They thought highly of this deed that Odd had done. Odd asked who it had been that he had avenged. They said that this man was the bishop. Odd said, 'Then it was better work than not doing it.' So now they kept an eye on Odd, because they did not in the least want him to go. But just as he had before been bored by being there, now things were worse since he found that they kept watch on him, and now he waited a chance to get away.

One night he got the chance and he ran away. He went from land to land, and came at last to the river Jordan. There he took off all his clothes including his shirt. Then he went into the river and washed himself as he pleased. Then he got out of the river and into his shirt, and it held all the magic as before. Now he went from there on out and he had his quiver on his back. Then he went still from land to land. Now he came to a wild forest and he had no other way to live but by shooting animals for food or birds, and so it went for a while.

CHAPTER EIGHTEEN

It is said that one day Odd came to a crag, and some big ravines, where a river fell in streams with much noise. He wondered how anyone could get across, and he saw no way. He sat down, and he had not been there long when something caught him up and lifted him into the air. A vulture had come flying at Odd and snatched him with its claws so fast that he could not protect himself against it. This creature flew with Odd across many lands and seas. But eventually it flew with him to some cliffs and landed on a grassy ledge. Here its young waited. When it let Odd loose, he was whole and unharmed, as his shirt had shielded him from the claws of this vulture as from all else that has already been mentioned.

Now Odd was left with the vulture's young in the nest. There was a high cliff above, while a sheer drop was underneath. Odd could see no way to get away without risking his life and jumping into the sea. But there seemed to be no chance of getting ashore anywhere and he saw no end to the cliffs. The chicks were still unfledged. The vulture was rarely home in the lair, and it was always looking for prey. Odd bound up the beaks of the young, but concealed himself in a rock cleft behind the nest. The vulture carried there more fish and birds and human flesh, and of all sorts of animals and livestock. It came about at last that it carried cooked meat there. But when the vulture goes away, Odd took the food, but concealed himself in between.

One day Odd saw a great giant rowing in a stone boat towards the nest. He shouted and said: 'An evil bird is nesting there, as he is accustomed to, steal away my freshly boiled meat day after day. I shall now seek to avenge myself somewhat. When I took the oxen of the king, I did not mean that a bird that would have them.' Odd stood up and killed the chicks, and called to the giant: 'Here is all that you are looking for, and I have taken care of it.' The giant went into the nest and took his meat and bore it to the boat. The giant said, 'Where is the little bairn that I saw here? Don't be scared, come out and go with me.' Odd showed himself then, and the giant took him and put him in the boat. He said: 'How shall I kill this monster?' Odd said, 'Set fire to the nest, and when the vulture comes back, I feel it may be that he will fly so near that fire will catch its feathers, and then we can kill it.' It happened as Odd said, and they defeated the vulture. Odd cut off its beaks and claws, and took them with him and climbed into the boat, and the giant rowed away.

Odd asked him his name, and he said he was called Hildir and he was one of the giants of Giantland and he had a wife called Hildirid, and with her a daughter named Hildigunn. 'And I have a son called Godmund and he was born yesterday. I am one of three brothers. The name of one is Ulf, the other Ylfing. We have arranged a meeting next summer to elect the person to be king of Giantland, who is to be the one who does the most remarkable deeds and has the most savage dog in the dogfight in the meeting.' Odd said, 'Who do you think out of you will become king?' Hildir answered: 'It seems to me that one of them will receive it, because I have always been the least of us, and so it will still be.' Odd said, 'What would you choose that would be best in this case?' Hildir answered: 'I would choose to be king, but it is however mighty unlikely, because Ulf has a wolf that is so fierce that no dog can tolerate him. Ulf has killed that animal called the tiger, and he has the head of the beast to prove it. But Ylfing, my brother, is, however, even harder, since he has an unbeatable polar bear. Ylfing has killed an animal that is called the unicorn, but I have no deeds to compare with theirs and no dog to compare either.'

'Well, it seems to me,' said Odd, 'that there would be a solution if someone applied himself, if a man was sympathetic.' Hildir said, 'I have never met a child as little as you, nor as arrogant as you nor as crafty, because I think it may turn out that even though you're too clever by half, you are the greatest treasure, and I will bring you Hildigunn, my daughter, and she can have you to play with and foster you and bring you up with Godmund, my son.'

After that Hildir set to the oars and rowed home to Giantland and Odd thought the boat went very fast. When he got home, he showed them the child that he had found, and asked his daughter to take care of this child with their own. Hildigunn took Odd and when he was with her, he stood close to her thighs, but Hildir was taller than her, as a man would be. But Hildigunn picked Odd up and put him on her knees, then she turned him to look at him, and said:

'This tiny pip

Has a tuft under his nose,

But Godmund is bigger,

Though born yesterday.'

She put him in a cradle with the giant baby and sang lullabies to the child and cuddled with them. But when he was restless in his cradle, she put him to bed with her and caressed him, and it came about that Odd played the games he wished and now things went well with them. Then Odd told her that he was not a child, though he was smaller than local men. But the people of Giantland are so much bigger and stronger than any other kind; friendly, they are handsome, but no wiser than most men.

Odd stayed there over the winter and in the spring he asked Hildir how generous he would be with a man who led him the dog that could beat his brothers'. Hildir answered 'I would oblige him. Can you get me something matching that description?' Odd said, 'Perhaps I can show you, but you should take it yourself.' Hildir answered, 'I will get him, but you show me it.' Odd said, 'An animal lies on Varg Island called a hibernating bear. Such is the nature of it that it lies asleep all winter, but in summer it gets up and then it is so greedy and cruel that nothing is safe, neither cattle nor men nor anything it meets. Now I think that this animal would beat your brothers' dogs.' Hildir said, 'Take me to this dog, and if it turns out as you say, then I will you pay well when I'm in power.' They got ready to go. Then Hildigunn spoke to Odd. 'Will you come back after this?' He said that he did not necessarily know. 'It would mean a lot to me,' she said, 'because I love you greatly, although you are small. We must not hide it from ourselves that I am with child, though it seems unlikely to think that you could do this, so small and feeble as you are. There is, however, no one except you who can be the father of the child that I carry. And though I love you very much, I do not mean to stop you going wherever you want, because I see that you do not have the character to be with us here any longer, but do not doubt it, you could not get away from here, unless I permit it. Now I will rather bear grief and sorrow and mourn here emptily, whatever happens, than you not be in the places that seem to you good. But what do you want me to do with our child?'

'You must,' said Odd, 'send him to me, if it's a boy, when he is ten years old, because I have hopes for him. But if it is a girl, then she should be brought up here, and look after her yourself, because I will not have anything to give her.'

'You shall have your own way in this as in everything else,' she said, 'between us, now farewell.' She cried bitterly, but Odd went to the ship.

Hildir rowed. To Odd it seemed he was too slow the oars, because the way was long. He resorted to the magic which Hrafnista men were given, and he hoisted the sails, and there came a fair wind, and they sailed out of the country and it was not long before Hildir got to his feet in the boat and went to Odd, seized him and knocked him down, and said: 'I will kill you if you don't stop this magic of yours, for the shore and mountains run past as if they are sheep, and the ship will sink under us.' Odd said, 'Do not think that, for you are dizzy because you're not accustomed to sailing; now let me stand up, and you will learn that I'm telling the truth.' He did as Odd asked. Odd reefed the sail; the shore and mountains were calm. Odd asked him not to wonder, however, if he saw this often when they sailed, and he said he could stop when he wished. Hildir was now calm after what Odd said, and he understood that this way was quicker than rowing; Odd hoisted the sails and sailed away, and Hildir was quiet.

There is nothing told of their journey until they came to Varg Islands and went ashore. There was a large scree slope. Odd asked Hildir to stretch his hand down among the stones and see if he could get something. He did so, and his arm went into the stones up to the shoulder, and said, 'Oh, here's something odd inside, and I will get my rowing glove,' and so he did and then pulled out a bear by the ears. Odd said, 'Now, treat this dog just as I said; take it home with you and don't let it loose earlier than at the meeting when you fight with the dogs. Do not feed it until the summer and keep it alone in the house and tell no one that you should have got it. But first day of summer, match it with your brothers' dogs, but if it's not enough, then come to this grim place another summer; I will then give more advice if this does not work.' Hildir had got bites all over his hands. He said, 'This I wish you to do, Odd, that you come to this grim place next spring but one, at this time.' Odd agreed to it.

Hildir went home with the animal and did everything Odd had said, but Odd went other way, and we cannot speak of his actions or accomplishments until the second spring when he went to the place where they had agreed to meet. Odd came first and went into the woods a short way from there and would not let Hildir see him, because he did not want to meet him, thinking that he would want revenge if everything had not gone according to what that he had told him. And not much later he heard the sound of oars and saw Hild come ashore, and in one hand had a cauldron full of silver, and in the other two very heavy chests. And he came to the place where they had promised to meet, then he waited there for some time, and there was no sign of Odd. Then said the giant, 'It is a shame now, Odd, foster son, that you did not come, but I see no point in staying here long, because my domain's leaderless while I am away, then I leave here these boxes, which are full of gold, and a cauldron full of silver; please have this treasure, even if you come later. I will put on top of it this flat stone so no wind blows them away, but if you cannot see it, I'm putting down these treasures, a sword, helmet and shield. But if you're any closer, so that you can hear my words, then I tell you that I was chosen king out of my brothers and I had a great savage dog because he bit to death both the dogs of my brothers and many of the men would rescue the dogs. I produced the beak and claws of a vulture, and it seemed a greater deed than those my brothers had achieved; I am now the king of the land that we three brothers had formerly. Now I will go back to my kingdom. Come to me, I shall give you the best of everything. I can also tell you that Hildigunn, my daughter, has given birth to a boy named Vignir, and she said that you fathered him upon her; I shall bring him up to be a lord. I will teach him sports and do all for him as I would for my own son, and when he is ten years old he will be sent to you, according to what you told her to do.' Then he rowed off in his craft. And when he had gone, Odd stood up and went to where the treasure was under the slab, but it was so big a rock that a crowd of people could not have stirred it. Odd could only reach the goods that lay on top of the slab, and they were worth a great deal of wealth. Having taken this treasure, Odd went on his way into the forest.

CHAPTER NINETEEN

One day Odd came to the edge of the forest. He was very tired, and he sat down under an oak. Then he saw a man walking past. He wore a blue-flecked cloak, high shoes, had a reed in his hand, and he had gold emblazoned gloves, was an average man in stature and genteel in appearance; a lowered hood covered his face. He had a big moustache and long beard, both of them red. He turned to Odd, where he sat, and greeted him by name. Odd welcomed him and asked who he was. He said he was Grani, called Raudgrani. 'I know all about you, Arrow-Odd,' he said, 'it seems to me good to hear, since you are the greatest hero and an accomplished man, but you have few followers, and travel rather like a pauper, and it is bad that a man like you should be so reduced.'

'It has been long now, though,' said Odd, 'that I have not been a leader of men.'

'Will you now swear an oath of brotherhood with me?' Raudgrani said. 'It's hard to deny such an offer,' said Odd, 'and I will take it up.'

'You are not yet wholly luckless,' said Raudgrani. 'Now I will tell you that there are two champions in the east of this country and they have twelve ships. They are sworn brothers; one comes from out of Denmark and is called Gardar, and the other Sirnir and comes out of Gautland. I know of no other heroes on this side of the sea and they do well at most things, and there I will bring you into brotherhood with them, yet you'll have the most say of us all, although following my advice will be best. But where would you want to sail if this is arranged as I have now said?'

'It is always in my mind that I would find Ogmund Eythjof's-Bane, who is called by another name, Tussock.'

'Stop, stop,' said Raudgrani, 'and don't say that, because he is not a man of humankind, is Ogmund, and if you meet Ogmund another time you will get from him far worse than before, so put this idea to find him from your mind.' Odd answered: 'One thing I wish to do is to avenge Thord, my blood brother, and I shall never give up until I can find him, if that is my fate.'

'Do you want me to tell you,' said Raudgrani, 'how Ogmund was born? If I do, you will see there is no chance that he will be killed by mortal men, if you know of his origin.

'Now is it told first in the tale that Harek was the name of a king who ruled Bjarmaland when you made your Viking raid, you will remember what damage you did to the Bjarmians. When you had gone away, they thought they had got a bad deal and would gladly take revenge, if they could. This was how they did it, they got a giantess who lived under a large waterfall, filled her with magic and sorcery, and laid her in bed with the king, and with her he had a son; the boy was sprinkled with water and given a name and called Ogmund. He was unlike most mortal men from an early age, as you'd expect from his mother, but his father was the greatest of men for sacrifices. When Ogmund was three years old, he was sent to Finnmark, and he studied all kinds of magic and sorcery, and when he was fully trained he went home to Bjarmaland. He was then seven years old and as big as a full grown man, very powerful and bad to deal with. His looks had not improved while he was with the Lapps' sons, because he was both black and blue, with his hair long and black, and a tussock hanging down over the eyes where a forelock should be. He was called Ogmund Tussock. They meant to send him to meet you and slay you; although they knew that much would need to be prepared before they could bring you death. It was next that they strengthened Ogmund with witchcraft, so that no normal iron should bite him. Subsequently they sacrificed to him and altered him so that he was no longer a mortal man.

'Eythjof was the name of a Viking. He was the greatest of berserks and an unparalleled hero, so that there did not seem to be any hero greater than him, and he never had fewer ships than eighteen when raiding. He never spent time on land and lay out on the sea, winter and hot summer. Everyone was scared of him wherever he went. He conquered Bjarmaland and forced them to pay tribute. Then Ogmund got eight comrades. They were all dressed in thick woollen cloaks, and no iron bit them. They were named thus: Hak and Haki, Tindall and Toki, Finn and Fjosni, Tjosni and Torfi. Then Ogmund joined up with Eythjof, and they went to war together. Ogmund was ten years old. He was with Eythjof for five winters. Eythjof was so fond of him that he could not refuse him anything, and for his sake he freed Bjarmaland from tribute. Ogmund rewarded Eythjof no better than to kill him sleeping in his bed and conceal the murder. It was easy to do because Eythjof had put him in the same bed with him, and not done anything against him, and he planned to make him his adopted son. He left Eythjof's men, and they went where they pleased, but Ogmund had two ships fully crewed. He was then called Ogmund Eythjof's Bane. And that same summer you fought him at Tronuvagar, and was Ogmund then fifteen years old. He hated getting no vengeance against you, and so he murdered Thord Prow-Gleam, your sworn brother. Then he went to meet the giantess, his mother, who was Grimhild when she was with humans. But then she was a *finngalkin*. She looks human as far as her head, but like an animal further down and has remarkably large claws and a tremendous tail, and with it she kills both humans and livestock, animals and dragons. Ogmund tried to get her to get you, and now she lives in the forests with animals and has reached the north of England and is looking at you. Now I have told you plainly of Ogmund.'

Odd said: 'It seems to me understandable why most men find him hard to fight, if he is as you say, but I still want to meet him.'

'Worse he is, though,' Raudgrani said, 'he is said to be more wraith than man, so I think that he will not be killed by any humans. But let us go down to the ships first,' - and so they did. And when they came to the sea, Odd saw where many ships floated. They went aboard. Odd saw two men who stood out from the rest. They stood up and greeted Raudgrani as their blood brother. He sat down between them and told Odd to sit. Raudgrani said, 'Here's a man who you sworn brothers will have heard told of, called Odd and Arrow-Odd. I wish that he be sworn our blood brother; he shall also be one to lead us, because he is most experienced in warfare.' Sirnir answered: 'Is he the Odd who went to Bjarmaland?'

'Yes,' said Raudgrani. 'We shall benefit,' said Sirnir, 'if he is sworn as our brother.'

'Full well I like it,' said Gardar. They bound this fast with promises. Then Raudgrani asked where Odd meant to go. 'Let us first,' said Odd, 'sail west to England.' So they did, that they sailed to the place, and when they came to the country they put up awnings over the ship, and lay there for a while.

CHAPTER TWENTY

One day of good weather Sirnir and Gardar went ashore for entertainment and many with them, but Odd stayed on the ship. Raudgrani was nowhere to be seen. The weather was surprisingly warm, and the sworn brothers took off their clothes and went swimming in a lake. There was a forest nearby. Most of the people were at some game or other. But as the day wore on, they saw that an incredibly large animal come out of the woods. It had a human head and immense fangs. Its tail was both long and stout, its claws remarkably large. It had a sword in each claw: they were both gleaming and big. When this *finngalkin* came out to the men, she howled menacingly at them and killed five men in the first attack. Two of them she cut down with a sword, a third she bit with her teeth, two she struck with her tail, and both died. Within a little time she had killed sixty people. Gardar dressed and stole out against the *finngalkin* and struck her with his sword so hard that one sword was knocked from her claws and into the lake, but she hit him with the other sword, so that he fell to the ground. Then she jumped on top of him. In came Sirnir with a sword that never failed, named Snidil, best of all blades, which never wavered in the fight. He struck the beast, and knocked the second sword into the water. The *finngalkin* trampled him under her, so that he was knocked out. Men who escaped ran to the ships and told Odd that the foster-brothers, and many others, had been killed and said that none of them could withstand monsters, - 'and please, Odd,' they said, 'sail immediately from this country, and save us as quickly as possible.'

'It would be a great shame,' said Odd, 'if we went away and I did not avenge the foster-brothers, such valiant men were they, and I'll never do it.' He took his quiver and went ashore. And when he had gone only a short way, he heard a terrifying noise. A little later Odd saw where the *finngalkin* was. He puts one of Gusir's Gifts to the bowstring, and shot it into the eye of the beast, and out the back of the head. The *finngalkin* went at him so hard that Odd could not use the bow. It clawed at his chest so hard that he fell on his back, but the shirt protected him as ever, so that the claws did not harm Odd. Swiftly he drew the sword he was girded with, and cut off the animal's tail when it was going to strike him, but he kept one hand out so that it could not bite at him. And when he had cut off her tail she ran to the wood screaming. Odd then shot another of Gusir's Gifts. It got the animal in the back, right in the heart and through the breast; the *finngalkin* then fell to the ground. Many people ran up to the animal then and hacked and hewed, who had not dared to come close before. The animal was utterly dead. Then Odd burnt the animal, and took the sworn brothers to the ship to be healed.

They went away from there and stayed in Denmark over the winter. They spent the following summers in raiding and fought in Sweden, Saxony, Frankland and Flanders until Sirnir and Gardar grew tired of raiding and settled down in their respective countries. Raudgrani followed them, for he had come down to the shore when they were ready to sail, after Odd had killed the *finngalkin*. Rarely was Raudgrani there when there was danger for people, but he was a great adviser when it was needed, and he rarely tried to stop them from performing great deeds.

CHAPTER TWENTY ONE

Odd went raiding and he had three ships well manned. He went again to seek Ogmund Eythjof's-Bane. Ten years had now passed since Odd left Giantland. One evening Odd lay off a headland and he had pitched a tent. He saw a man rowing in a boat. Whoever it was was rowing powerfully, and he was amazingly big to see. He rowed so hard up to Odd's ships that everything was broken before him. Then he went ashore, to where the tent was, and asked who was in charge. Odd said to him, - 'Who are you?' He said he was named Vignir - 'Odd, are you the one who went to Bjarmaland?'

'It is true, that,' said Odd. 'I am speechless,' said Vignir. 'Why so?' said Odd. 'Because,' said Vignir, 'I can barely believe that you're a father to me, so small and weak-looking as you seem to be.'

'Who is your mother?' Odd said, 'And how old are you?'

'My mother is called Hildigunn,' said Vignir; 'I was born in Giantland, and I was brought up there,

THE SAGA OF ARROW-ODD

but now I'm ten years old. My mother told me that Arrow-Odd was my father, and I was thinking he would be a real man, but now I see that you are the least of nobodies to look at, and so you will turn out to be.' Odd said: 'Do you think that you will do more or work greater feats than I have? But I will accept my kinship with you and you're welcome to remain with me.'

'That I will, and I accept it,' said Vignir, 'but it seems to me, however, very demeaning to be mixed with you and your men, because I think they more closely resemble mice than men, and it seems to me very likely that I will do bigger things than you, if I live long.' Odd asked him not to insult his men.

In the morning they got ready to sail. Then Vignir asked Odd where he would sail. He said he wanted to look for Ogmund Eythjof's-Bane. 'From him, you'll get no good, if you find him,' said Vignir, 'because he is the greatest troll and monster ever created in the northern part of the world.'

'It cannot be true,' said Odd, 'that when you mock my stature and my men, you are now so scared that you dare not seek or find Ogmund Tussock.'

'No need,' said Vignir, 'to taunt me with cowardice, but I will repay you for your words some time, so that it will seem to you no better than this does to me now. But I will tell you where Ogmund is. He's in the fjord named Skuggi, in Helluland's wastes[6], and his nine tussocked lads with him. He went there because he cannot be bothered finding you. Now, you may visit him, if you want, and see how it goes.' Odd said it should be so.

Then they sailed till they came to the Greenland Sea, then turned south and west along the coast. Then Vignir said: 'Now I shall sail in my boat today, but you can follow after.' Odd let him go his own way. Vignir was master of one ship. They saw that day where two rocks emerged from the sea. Odd wondered much at that. They sailed between the cliffs. But as the day wore on, they saw a huge island. Odd asked them to sail up to it. Vignir asked why. Odd asked five men to go ashore and seek water. Vignir said there was no need, and he said none of his ship were going. But when Odd's men came to the island, they had been there only a little while before the island sank and drowned them all. The island was covered with heather. They did not see it again. When they also looked at the rocks, they saw they had vanished. Odd was very surprised by this, and asked Vignir why this was. Vignir said: 'It seems to me that you have no more sense than stature. Now I will tell you that these are two sea monsters. One is named Hafgufa, the other Lyngbak. The latter is the greatest of all whales in the world, but Hafgufa is the biggest of monsters created in the ocean. It is her nature that she swallows both men and ships and whales and all that she can reach. She stays submerged day and night together, and then she lifts up her head and nostrils, then it is never less time than the tide that she stays up. Now that sound that we sailed through was the gap between her jaws, and her nose and lower jaw were the rocks you saw in the ocean, but Lyngbak was the island that sank[7]. Ogmund Tussock has sent these creatures to you with his enchantments to work the death of you and all your men. He thought that this would have killed more men than those that drowned, and he meant that Hafgufa would swallow us whole. Therefore I sailed through her mouth because I knew that she had just risen to the surface. Now we have seen through these contrivances of Ogmund, but it is my thinking that we will suffer from him worse than any other men.'

'That's a risk we're going to have to take,' said Odd.

CHAPTER TWENTY TWO

Now they sailed until they came to Helluland and into the fjord called Skuggi. But when they had moored, father and son went ashore and to a spot they saw where a fortress stood, and it seemed that it was a well-defended place. Ogmund went out on one of the walls with his companions. He greeted Odd blithely and asked them their errand. 'You do not need to ask,' Odd said, 'because I want your life.'

'The other idea is better,' said Ogmund, 'that we accept full settlement.'

'No,' said Odd, 'that will not be, because the first idea has been in my mind since you had Thord Prow-Gleam, my blood brother, so shamefully killed.'

'I only did that,' said Ogmund, 'because we did not have equal numbers of slain, but now if you've caught up with me, you will never defeat me while I am in the fort, but now I offer you, that either you two fight me and my companions, or we stay in the fort.'

'It must be,' said Odd, 'and I will fight with you Ogmund, and Vignir will fight your companions.'

'That shall not be,' said Vignir, 'I will now reward you for your taunting words that you said to me the first time that we first met, that I would not dare encounter Ogmund.'

'We'll regret this arrangement later,' said Odd, 'though now you get your own way.'

Then they started fighting. It was a close thing. It was some hard fighting that Ogmund and Vignir underwent, because both their strength and power was the same as was their weapon skill. And Vignir pressed Ogmund so hard he ran northwards along the sea cliff, but Vignir ran after him until Ogmund ran down over the rocks onto a grassy ledge, but after him came Vignir; they were forty fathoms above sea level. Then they met and were faced with a great struggle and bitter, because they tore up the earth and stones like loose snow. Now we go back to Odd. He had a big club in his hand, because iron bit none of the Tussock boys. He hit about him hard with a club so that in a moment he had killed them all. He was weary, but he was unhurt; this was caused by his shirt. Odd decided he should look after Vignir, and learn from him what had happened. He went along the cliff edge until he came up to that place above where Vignir and Ogmund had been fighting. And at that point Ogmund surprised Vignir so that he fell, and as soon as he did he bent down over him and bit out his throat. Vignir was dead. Odd said that sight was the worst he had ever seen, and most saddening. Ogmund said: 'Now, I think, Odd, it would have been better that we had settled as I asked, because now you have got a loss from me that you'll never recover from, as your son Vignir is dead, a man that I think would have been the most valiant and strongest of all in the northern lands, for he was now ten years old, and he would have gained victory if I was an ordinary man, but now I more a wraith than a man. And he violently crushed my body and he has near enough broken everything in me, every bone, so that they all scrape within the skin, so that I would be dead if it was in my nature to do so, but I am afraid of no one in this world except you, and from you I will get my own ill fortune, sooner or later, because now you have more reason for revenge.' Odd then became wildly angry, and then he jumped down the cliff, and landed down on the ledge. Ogmund moved himself quickly and threw himself down the rocks into the sea head first, so that sea spray surged up the cliff. There was no sign of Ogmund again so far as Odd could see. Then they parted this time, and Odd felt the worst of it, and then he went to the ships and sailed away. He went to Denmark and found Gardar, his foster-brother, and he gave Odd a warm welcome.

CHAPTER TWENTY THREE

Odd stayed in Denmark that winter, but when spring came he and Gardar went to war and they sent word to Sirnir in Gautland. He went to meet them, and with him went Raudgrani. Raudgrani asked Odd where he wanted to go. He said he wanted to seek Ogmund Eythjof's-Bane and continue the search for him. 'It seems to me that you seek sorrow,' said Raudgrani, 'you keep looking after Ogmund, but every time that you meet, you get from him both shame and wretchedness, and there's no need to think that Ogmund has changed since you parted. But I can tell you where he's gone, if you are interested. He went east to the giant Geirrod[8] in Geirrodargard and he has married Geirrid, his daughter, and both are the worst of trolls, and I wouldn't advise you to go there.' Odd said he would go anyway.

Then they all made ready, the sworn brothers,

to go east, and when they came to Geirrodargard, they saw where a man was sitting in a boat to fish. It was Ogmund Eythjof's Bane indeed, and he had on a shaggy cape. When he had separated with Odd, he had gone away to the east and become son-in-law of Geirrod the giant, and he took tribute from all the kings of the Baltic in such a way that they would send him every twelve months their beards and moustaches. Ogmund had made of them the same coat that he wore. Odd and his men headed towards the boat, but Ogmund retreated; he rowed rather strongly. The sworn brothers all jumped into a boat and rowed after him furiously, but Tussock rowed so mightily that they kept the same distance until that they came to land. Then Ogmund ran ashore leaving his boat on the strand. Odd was the fastest of the men to get ashore and he was followed by Sirnir, and both ran after Ogmund. But Ogmund when saw that they would catch up, he spoke, and recited:

'I pray to Geirrod

For the gods' favour,

Greatest of warriors,

Grant me assistance

And my wife

Quickly to others,

I need now all

The aid they can give.'

Then the old saying was proved true, that if you speak of the devil, he's sure to appear. Geirrod came there with all his people, and there were fifty of them in all. Then came Gardar and Odd's men. They entered into the hardest battle. Geirrod hit rather hard, so in a little time he had killed fifteen men of Odd's. Odd then looked for Gusir's Gifts. He took Hremsu and laid it on the bowstring and shot. It hit Geirrod in the breast and came out at the shoulders. Geirrod still came on even after taking the arrow, and he killed three men before he fell dead to the ground. Geirrid was also a threat because she killed eighteen men in a small time. Gardar turned to her and they traded blows, but it ended that Gardar was beaten dead to the ground. When Odd saw that, he was tremendously angry. So he put one of Gusir's Gifts to the string and shot it into the right armpit of Geirrid and it came out of the left. As far as anyone could tell it did nothing to her. Then she rushed into the battle, and killed five people. Odd then shot another of Gusir's Gifts. It came into her small intestine and out of her thighs; she died soon after.

Ogmund also did not waste time in battle, since he had killed thirty men in a short while before Sirnir turned towards him, and they had a hard fight, and Sirnir was quickly wounded. A little later, Odd saw that Sirnir retreated from Ogmund. He turned that way, but when Ogmund saw that, he turned and fled and ran in disorder rather foolishly, but Sirnir and Odd went after him. Both of them were running very fast. Ogmund wore his fine coat well, but when they were almost level with him, Ogmund threw down the cloak and recited:

'Now must I cast

Away my cloak,

Which was made

Of kings' moustaches,

Embroidered with them

On both sides,

I am very grieved

To give it up.

They pursue me

At full pelt,

Odd and Sirnir,

From the encounter.'

But now that Ogmund was lighter clad, he pulled away. Odd hardened himself then, and he ran quicker than Sirnir. And when Ogmund saw that, he turned towards him, and they got to grips.

They were wrestling and fighting both hard and long, since Odd was not as powerful as Ogmund, but Ogmund could not knock him off his feet. Then Sirnir came up with a drawn sword, Snidil, intending to strike at Ogmund, but when Ogmund saw that he turned and thrust Odd between himself and the blow. Then Sirnir held back. So it went, that Ogmund used Odd a shield and Sirnir could do nothing, but even when Odd was hit, he was not wounded because of his good shirt. And at one point, Odd braced both feet against a solid stone sunk in the earth so hard that Ogmund was brought to his knees. Sirnir hacked at Ogmund. Then he had no opportunity to parry the blow with Odd. It hit him in the buttocks, and took a slice. Sirnir cut so great a piece out of Ogmund's backside that no horse could carry more. This worried Ogmund so that he sank down into the earth where he was. Odd grabbed his beard with both hands, with so much force that he tore it from him and beard and skin down to the bone, and all the face with both cheeks, and so it went on up the forehead and the middle of the crown, and they went their ways as the ground opened, but Odd kept what he held. The earth closed above the head of Ogmund, and so they parted.

Odd and Sirnir returned to their ships, and they had experienced considerable loss of life. Odd thought it was the greatest sorrow that he had lost Gardar, his foster-brother. Raudgrani was also gone, and Odd and Sirnir never learnt what became of him after they found Ogmund in the boat. It was true that he himself seldom faced danger, but he gave the toughest advice. The sworn brothers never Raudgrani again, it is told. Men think he may have actually been Odin. The sworn brothers went away, and it seemed to people that Odd had still not got the better of Ogmund, having lost Gardar, his foster-brother, a high-spirited man who had helped Odd and achieved a lot by killing those monsters who were with Ogmund. Geirrid had a son by Ogmund Eythjof's-Bane, named Svart. He was three years old when he came into the story. He was tall and it looked likely that he would turn into an evil man.

CHAPTER TWENTY FOUR

Odd returned to Gautland with his blood brother, Sirnir, who invited him to stay for the winter. Odd accepted. And as the winter wore on, he became very depressed. To his mind came the miseries he had got from Ogmund Tussock. He did not ever want to risk his blood brother's life in the fight with Ogmund, because he thought he had suffered losses enough already. It then became his plan to steal away alone at night. He then got transport where he needed, but he travelled through wildernesses, and forests, and ran along long mountain paths. He had the quiver on his back. He went now through many countries, and it came about at last that he had to shoot birds for his food. He folded birch bark round his body and feet. Then he made a big hat with the bark. He was not like other men, far bigger than any other, and he was all covered in bark.

Now nothing is told about him before he came out from the forest, and he saw settlements before him. He saw that a great farm stood there, but there was another farm close by. It came into his mind that he would try the smaller farm; though he had never previously tried anything like that. He went up to the door. There was a man at the door chopping wood. The man was small in size and white-haired. He welcomed him, and asked the man his name. 'My name is Barkman,' he said, 'but what is your name?' He was called Jolf. 'You would like to stay the night,' said the man. 'That I would,' said Barkman. Now he followed the man into his living room, where his wife sat alone on a chair. 'Here is a visitor,' said the old man, 'you shall entertain him, I have many things to do.' The old woman grumbled a lot, and said that he often offered people accommodation, - 'but there is nothing to give him.' Now the man went away, but the woman sat with Odd. And at evening, when Jolf came in, there was a table set for them with one dish, but on the side Barkman sat, he put down a good knife. Two rings were on the knife, one of gold, the other of silver. When Jolf saw it, he reached for his knife and examined it. 'You have a good knife, mate,' said the man, 'how did you come by this treasure?' Barkman said: 'When I was at a young age, we made salt together and one day a ship was wrecked near where we were. The ship was broken to pieces, and the men were washed ashore, and were very weak, and we quickly finished them off, and I got a knife in my share of the plunder, but if you, man, have any use for it, then I will give you the knife.'

'Best of luck to you,' said the man and he showed the woman his knife. 'This is good,' he said, 'and see this knife is nothing worse than the one I had before.' After that they had their food, and then what followed was Barkman went to sleep, and slept through the night, and he did not wake until Jolf was away, and his bed was cold. Then he said, 'Will it not be best for me to get up and go out and look for breakfast elsewhere?' The old woman said that the old man wanted him to stay in his home.

It was near the middle of the day when the man came, and the Barkman was on his feet. Then the table was laid. There was a dish on the board, the old man put down beside him three arrows with stone heads. These were large arrows and fair, so Barkman thought he had never seen that kind of arrow. He took one up and looked at it. 'This arrow is well made,' he said. 'If you think,' said the old man, 'you like them, then I will give them to you.' Barkman smiled at him and said, 'I am not sure there's any reason for me to carry these stone arrows along with me.'

'That you'll never know, Odd,' said the man, 'when you might need them. I know that you are called Arrow-Odd and are the son of Grim Hairycheek from north in Hrafnista. I know, too, that you have three arrows called Gusir's Gifts, and you will think it strange, when you come to a time when Gusir's Gifts fail you and these arrows save you.'

'Since you know that my name is Odd, and also that I have the arrows named Gusir's Gifts, it could be,' said Odd, 'that you are right, what you said before. I shall certainly accept the arrows,' and he put them in his quiver. 'What do you say, man,' said Odd, 'about this land? Is there a king?'

'Yes,' said the man, 'and he is called Herraud.'

'Who is the noblest men with him?' said Odd. 'There are two men,' said the man, 'one called Sigurd, and the other Sjolf. They are the chief men of the king, and the best of all fighters.'

'Who are the king's children?' said Odd. 'He has one beautiful daughter called Silkisif.'

'She's a beautiful woman?' said Odd. 'Yes,' said the man, 'there is none other as beautiful in Gardariki and elsewhere.'

'Tell me, man,' said Odd, 'how they'll receive me, if I go there? And do not tell them who I am.'

'I can hold my tongue,' said the man.

Then they went to the royal hall. Then the old man put his foot down and refused to go further. 'Why do you stop?' said Odd. 'Because,' said the man, 'I will be put in shackles if I go in here, and I will be happier when I get off.'

'No,' said Barkman, 'we shall both go in together, and I cannot settle for anything but that you go,' and clutched him. Then they entered the hall. When the king's retainers saw the old man, they mobbed him, but Barkman supported him, so that they bounced off. Now they went along the hall, so that they came to the king. The old man greeted the king politely. The king took it well. Then the king asked whom he brought along with him. 'It may be that I can't say,' said the man, 'and so he must tell you that himself.'

'My name is Barkman,' he said. 'Who are you, mate?' said the king. 'This I know,' he said, 'I am older than anything you know, but there is neither wit nor memory in my skull, and I have lived outside in the forest of almost all my life. Beggars always want to be choosers, O king, and I ask you for winter lodgings.' The king replied, 'Are you at all skilled?'

'No,' he said, 'Because I am clumsier than other men.'

'Will you work a little?' said the king. 'I do not work, since I can't be bothered to work,' said Barkman. 'Then it looks unpromising,' said the king, 'for I have made a vow to take only men who are at all skilled.'

'Nothing I ever do,' said Barkman, 'will benefit anyone.'

'You must know how to collect game, when they go shooting,' said the king. 'It may be that I will go hunting sometime.'

'Where do you want me to sit?' Barkman said. 'You should sit farther out on the lower bench, between slaves and freedmen.' Now Barkman saw the old man out and after that went to the seat he had been offered. There were two brothers. One was named Ottar, the other Ingjald. 'Come here, mate,' they said, 'and you shall sit between us,' and that he did. They sat close at his knees on either side, and asked him about other lands that came to mind, but no one else knew what they were talking about. He hung up his quiver on a peg above him, but the club under his feet. They always asked him to take away the quiver, and it seemed to be a great nuisance, but he said he would never let it be taken away from him, and he went nowhere but he would he have it with him. They offered him bribes to take off the bark, 'and we will give you good clothes,' they said. 'That may not be so,' he said, 'because I have never worn anything else, and while I live I never will.'

CHAPTER TWENTY FIVE

Now Barkman sat there and generally he drank a little in early evening and then lay down to sleep. So it went on, till the men began to go hunting. It was autumn. Now Ingjald said one evening, - 'we must get up early in the morning.'

'Why is that?' Barkman said. Ingjald said they were going hunting. Then they lay down to sleep that evening, but in the morning the brothers rose and called to Barkman and they could not wake him, he was fast asleep, and he did not wake up until every man who would go hunting was gone. Barkman spoke and said: 'What is happening now, are they all ready?' Ingjald answered, 'Ready,' he said, 'but all the men are away, and we tried to wake you all morning, and we will never shoot any animals today.' Then Barkman 'Are they very great sportsmen, Sjolf and Sigurd?'

'We would know that,' said Ingjald, 'if ever anyone competed against them.' They came to the mountain, and a herd of deer ran past them, and the brothers drew their bows, and they tried shooting the deer, but missed each time. Then Barkman 'I have never seen,' he said, 'anyone do as badly as you do, and why do you made such a poor try at it?' They said: 'We have already told you that we are clumsier than others, but we were late getting ready in the morning and now the animals we meet are those others have already stirred up.' Barkman said: 'I do not believe that I could be worse than you, now give the bow here, and I will try.' Now they did so. He drew the bow, and they told him not to break it, but he pulled the arrow to the tip and the bow snapped into two pieces. 'Now you have done badly,' they said, 'and it has done us much damage. It is now unlikely that we will shoot any deer today.'

'Things have not gone well,' he said, 'but do you think my stick will work as a bow, and do you not both feel some curiosity to know what's in my bag?'

'Yes,' they said, 'we are pretty curious.'

'Then you spread your thick cloaks, and I will empty out what is in it.' So they did, and he threw down the bag's contents on the cloaks. Then he drew his bow and put an arrow to the string, and shot it over the heads of all the men that were at the hunt. So he did all day, shooting at the deer that Sigurd and Sjolf were going for. He shot all his arrows except six, the stone arrows he got from the old man, and Gusir's Gifts. He did not miss a deer that day, and the brothers ran with him, and great was their joy to see his shooting.

But in the evening, when the men came home, all people's arrows were brought to the king, and each man had marked his arrow, and the king saw how many deer each man had killed during the day. Now the brothers said, 'Go there, Barkman, after your arrows, on the table before the king.'

'You go,' he said, 'and say you both own the arrows.'

'They will not believe us,' they said, 'the king knows that as sportsmen we can hardly shoot like other men.'

'Then we shall all go together,' he said. Now they went before the king. Then Barkman said, 'Here are the arrows which we fellows claim.' The king looked at him and said: 'You are a great archer.'

'Yes, sire,' he said, 'because I am used to shooting animals and birds to eat.' And after that they went to their seats. Now time passed.

CHAPTER TWENTY SIX

One evening, when the king had gone to bed, Sigurd and Sjolf rose up and went with a horn to offer drink to the brothers, Ottar and Ingjald, and asked them to take it and drink from it. And when they had drunk, they came with another two, and they took them and drank. Then Sjolf, 'Does he always lie down, your associate?'

'Yes,' they said, 'he thinks it better than drinking himself senseless like we do.' Then Sjolf: 'Is he a good archer?'

'Yes,' they said, 'it is his gift as well as many other things.'

'Do you think he can shoot as well as both of us?' Sjolf said. 'As we see it,' said they, 'he will shoot much farther and straighter.'

'We must bet on it,' said Sjolf, 'and we will make the stake a bracelet worth half a mark, but you shall stake two rings of equal weight.' So it was agreed that the king should be there, and his daughter, would see their shooting, and they should take the bracelets before and give them to whoever the winner was, and then they laid their wager. They slept through the night. But the next morning, when the brothers woke up, it came to their minds that they had made fools of themselves over the bet, and they told Barkman. 'The bet seems to me to be unpromising,' he said, 'because even though I can shoot deer, it is but little compared with competing with such great archers, but I will try all the same since you have staked all your wealth.'

Now the men had drinks, and after drinks people went out, and now the king wanted to see the shooting. Now Sigurd went out and shot as far as he could, and a pole was placed in the ground, and Sjolf went up to it. A spear was put haft down and placed on top of it was a gold chessman, and Sjolf hit the chessman, and it seems to everyone that this was excellent shooting and he said that Barkman need not bother trying to compete. 'Good luck often alters bad,' said Barkman, 'and I'm going to try.' Now Barkman shot a single arrow, and stood where Sigurd had stood. He shot up in the air, so that the arrow remained out of sight for a long time, but when it came down, it went straight through the middle of the chessman, and into the spear shaft so that it did not move. 'As good as the shot was last time,' said the king, 'the shooting is now much better, and I can say that I have never seen such shooting.' Now Barkman took another arrow and shot so far that no one could see where it came down, and it was now agreed that he had won the game. After that, they went home, and the brothers were given the bracelet. They offered it to Barkman. He said he wanted their treasure to remain as things stand.

Now, some days later, another evening, the king had gone, and Sigurd and Sjolf went with a horn each which they offered to Ottar and Ingjald. They drank from them. Then they brought them another two. Then Sjolf, 'Still Barkman lies there and doesn't drink.'

'He is still better mannered than you in everything,' said Ingjald. 'I think there's more to it,' said Sjolf, 'that he will have rarely ever mixed with noble men, and he will have lain often out in the woods like a poor man, but does he swim well?'

'We expect he is good at most sports,' they say, 'and we think he's a very good swimmer.'

'Would he swim better than both of us?'

'We think that he is a better swimmer,' said Ottar. 'Here we will lay a bet on it,' said Sjolf, 'and we will stake a bracelet worth a mark, but you shall stake two rings, each a mark in weight.' Now it was so agreed that the king and his daughter should see their swimming contest, and it was all ordered as it was the first time. They slept through the

THE SAGA OF ARROW-ODD

night. In the morning, when they woke up, news of their bet had gone round the benches. 'What's this they're saying?' Barkman said. 'That you accepted another bet last night?'

'Yes,' they said, and then they told him all about the bet. 'Now I think it looks unpromising,' said Barkman, 'for I am not a swimmer, and I cannot stay afloat when I try, and it's a long time since I came into contact with cold water, and have you wagered much money?'

'Yes,' they said, 'but you don't have to try, unless you wish. It would be right if we had to pay for our foolishness.'

'That shall never be,' said Barkman, 'that I should not try, since you treat me with great honour, and the king and Silkisif will see that I will certainly go for a swim.'

Now the king was told, and his daughter, and now people went to the water, and it was a big lake and close by. When they came to the water the king and his retinue sat down and the competitors went swimming in their clothes, but Barkman wore the guise that he was accustomed to. They swam to him when they came from the shore, and tried to push him under and held him down for a long time. Then they let him come up, and took a rest. They ganged up on him a second time. He reached for them and took them in each hand, and forced them down and held them down so long that it seemed unlikely that they would come up again. He gave them a short rest and took them a second time and held them under, and for a third time and held them down so long that no one thought that they would arise alive. But they still came up, and then out of the nostrils came blood from both these excellencies of the stock of kings, and they needed to be helped back on land. Then Barkman took them and cast them ashore. Then he went swimming and played a lot of games, and the troop was glad to play at swimming. But in the evening he went ashore to meet the king. And then the king asked: 'Are you not a better sportsman than the rest, both at shooting and swimming?'

'You have now seen all my skill that I have,' said Barkman, 'my name is Odd, if you want to know that, but I will not tell you anything about my family.' Now Silkisif gave him the bracelets. Then they went home. Then the brothers said that Odd should have all the rings, but he refused it, - 'and you shall have them for yourselves.' Then time passed, but not long. The king was very anxious about who the man who was there with him might be.

CHAPTER TWENTY SEVEN

A man named Harek was there with the king. He had great respect from him. He was an old man and he had fostered the king's daughter. The king would talk to him about this issue, but he said he did not know and said he thought it likely that the man would came from a noble family. It happened one evening, when the king had gone to bed, that Sjolf and Sigurd went up to the brothers and they brought two horns, and they drank from them. Then Sjolf said, 'Does the great Odd sleep?'

'Yes,' they say, 'it is more sensible than drinking yourself witless like we do.'

'That could be because he is more used to lying out in the forest or lakes than to drinking well with people, or is he a great drinker?'

'Yes,' they say. 'Would he be a better drinker than us both?' Sjolf said. 'It seems to us,' said Ottar, 'he drinks a lot more.'

'We must bet on it,' said Sjolf, 'and we'll stake this bracelet, which stands at twelve ounces, but you shall stake your own heads.' They bound this agreement with them as they had in the past. Now that morning Odd asked what was said. They told him. 'Now you've really made a dumb bet,' said Odd, 'that what you have now increases the stakes from what they were formerly, since now you risk your heads, but it is not certain that I shall be the greater drinker though I am bigger than the others, but I will take them on when I go to the drinking match.' Then the king was told that he wanted to compete as a drinker, and the king's daughter was to sit in and watch, and Harek, her foster father. Now Sigurd and Sjolf went up to Odd. 'Here is a horn,' said Sigurd, and poetry came to his lips:

'Odd, you've never

Been in the fight

When helmeted troops fled,

Burst mail shirts;

Battle raged,

Fire blazed in the town,

When our king won,

Victorious, against the Wends.'

Sjolf brought him another horn, and told him to drink it and recited:

'Odd, we didn't see you

At the sword clash,

We dealt the king's forces

Death on a plate;

I took sword cuts,

Six and eight,

But you were begging

Your food from boors.'

Then they went to their seats, but Odd got up and went before Sigurd, and brought him a horn, another to Sjolf and recited a verse to each of them before he went away:

'I shall serve to

You my song

Sigurd and Sjolf,

Seat companions,

You both need payback

For such ornate poetry

A couple of pansies,

Are the pair of you.

You were, Sjolf,

On the kitchen floor

Deeds lacking,

Undaring cowards

And out in

Aquitania

Four people

Had I felled.'

They drank from the horns, but Odd went to sit down. Then they went over to Odd, and Sjolf gave him his horn and recited:

'*You, Odd, have been*

With beggars

And received titbits

From the table,

And I alone

From Ulfsfell

My hacked shield

Held in my hand.'

Sigurd brought him another horn and said this:

'Odd, we glimpsed you not

Out with the Greeks,

Fighting the Saracens

We reddened our swords;

We made the hard

Sound of harrying,

Felled the fighters,

The folk in red.'

Odd now drank from the horns, but they went to sit down. Then Odd rose and went with his horn to each of them and said this:

'You were giggling, Sjolf,

With the girlies,

While keen flames

Played through the fort;

We killed the hard

Hadding there,

And Olvir later his

Life we took.

You, Sigurd, lay

In the lady's bower,

While we battled

The Bjarmians twice;

Warlike heroes

With hawk like minds,

While you slumbered in the hall,

Slept under a sheet.'

Now Odd went to sit down, but they drank from the horn, and men thought it a great entertainment, and had given a good hearing so far. After that they went before Odd and brought him two horns. Whereupon Sjolf:

'*Odd, we saw you not*

On Atalsfjalli,

When the fen-fire

We had gathered;

We the berserks

Bound up there,

Of the king's troop many

A warrior was killed.'

Odd now drank from the horns, but they sat down. Odd brought them a horn and said this:

'Sjolf, you weren't seen,

Where you could see

Men's byrnies

Washed in blood;

Spear tips dug

In ring-sarks,

But in the king's hall

You'd rather cavort.

Sigurd, you weren't seen,

When we cleared six

High-pooped ships

Of Hauksnes;

You weren't seen

West of England,

When Skolli and I

Shortened the king's stay.'

Odd sat down now, but they brought him the horn and with no poetry. He drank of it, but they settle down. And now Odd brought them horns and said this:

'Sjolf, you weren't seen,

When we reddened our swords

Sharp on the Earl

Off Laeso island;

But you bunked down there

At home, torn between

The cuddlesome

Calf and the slave girl.

Sigurd, you weren't seen,

When on Zealand I slew

The battle-hard brothers,

Brand and Agnar,

Asmund, Ingjald,

Alf was the fifth;

But you were couched

In the hall of the king

Teller of tall tales,

A comic turn.'

Now he went to sit down, they stood up and brought him two horns. Odd drank them both. Then he brought them horns and said this:

'Sjolf, we saw you not

South at Skida,

Where noble kings

Knocked helmets;

Rapidly with blood,

We became ankle deep;

I was slaying men,

We saw you not there.

Sigurd, we saw you not

At Svia Skerries,

When we paid Halfdan

For his hospitality;

Our swords hacked

Battle-hewn shields,

Swords sliced,

He died himself.'

Now Odd sat down, but they brought him the horns and he drank them off, but they went to sit down. Odd then brought them the horns and said:

'*We sailed our ash-ship*

Through Elfar Sound,

Content and happy,

At Tronuvagar;

There was Ogmund

Eythjof's Bane,

Tardy to flee,

With two ships.

Then we showered

Linden shields

With hard stones

And sharp swords;

Three of us survived

But nine of them.

Captive rogue,

Why so quiet now?'

Odd then went to his seat, but they brought him two horns. He drank from them and offered them two more and said this:

'*Sigurd, we saw you not*

On Samsey island,

When we received

Strokes from Hjorvard;

Two of us,

But twelve of them;

I seized victory,

You sat quietly.

I went over Gautland

Grim in mind

Seven days I went,

Until I met Saemund;

I took then,

Before I travelled,

Eighteen people's

Lives away,

But you took – you

Pitiful wretch,

Late at the sunset –

A slave girl to bed.'

Then there was a great cheer in the hall at what Odd had sung, and they drank from their horns, but Odd sat down. The king's men enjoyed their entertainment. Once they brought Odd two horns, and he finished quickly both of them. After that Odd stood up and went to them and he thought that now that the drink and all had defeated them. He gave them the horns and said this:

'*You will never*

Be thought worthy,

Sigurd and Sjolf,

Company for a king;

Of Hjalmar I think,

The brave,

Who briskly swung

His sharp sword.

Thord was sharper

Who broke shields,

When we were in conflict

The heroic king;

He laid Halfdan

Upon the earth,

And all of his

Fellows and allies.

We were together, Asmund,

Often in childhood

Sworn brothers together

Many a time;

I often bore

In battle a spear,

Where kings

ANONYMOUS AUTHOR

Clashed in the fray.

We smote the Saxons

And raided the Swedes,

Ireland and England

And once Scotland

Frisians and Franks

And to say anything;

Smote them all

I was like a pestilence.

Now I'll list

All of them;

Those fierce warriors

Who followed me there;

Will never again

Will then never

See in battle

The brave people.

Now I've listed

All the deeds,

That long ago we

Had done;

We returned,

Pride of place,

To sit in our high seats;

Let Sjolf speak.'

After that Odd sat in his seat, but the brothers fell down and now there was no more of them in the drinking, but Odd drank for a long time, and after that they lay down and slept the night.

In the morning when the king came to the throne, Odd and his comrades were already up outside. He went at once to the water to wash. The brothers saw that the bark cuff was torn on one of his hands, and there was a red arm and gold rings on the arm, and they were not narrow. And then they ripped off all his bark. He did not try to stop this, but underneath he was clad in a scarlet robe of costly stuff, but his hair lay down to the shoulders. He had a golden band on his forehead and he was the most handsome of all men. They took his hands and led him into the house to the throne of the king, and said: 'It seems that we did not fully appreciate whom we have had here in our care.'

'It may be,' said the king, 'and who is this man who has so hidden his identity from us?'

'I am named Odd, which I told you months ago, son of Grim Hairycheek from northern Norway.'

'Are you not the Odd who travelled to Bjarmaland a long time ago?'

'He is the man who has come here.'

'It is not strange that my nobles did badly with you in sports.' The king now stood up and welcomed Odd well and invited him to sit on the throne with him. 'I will not take it like that, unless I go with my comrades.' It is said that they now changed their seats and Odd sat next to the king, but Harek moved from his place to a stool before the king. The king showed much respect to Odd, and he valued no man more than him.

CHAPTER TWENTY EIGHT

Odd and Harek often discussed things with each other. Odd inquired if men had not ask to marry the king's daughter. 'It is a fact,' he said, 'Both leading men have asked her for wife.'

'How did he answer this matter?' said Odd. 'He has said there is a chance,' he said. 'Let me hear about it,' said Odd. 'The king wants to collect tribute from a land named Bjalka. It is ruled by the king who is called Alf and nicknamed Bjalki. He is married. His wife is called Gydja. He is a great man for sacrifices and both are the same. They have a son together, called Vidgrip. They are such magicians that they could hitch a horse to a star. The king has tribute to collect from there, and it has long been unpaid. The king said that he would marry his daughter to the man who could collect the tribute from that land but it amounted to nothing, because they asked to go with so large a force to the country, the king thought he wouldn't have enough warriors to defend his realm.'

'So it seems to me,' said Odd, 'that either the tribute won't be gathered, or else that it must be gathered with a smaller force, but do you think the king will want to give me such a chance as the others, if I can retrieve the tribute?' said Odd. 'A wise man is the king,' said Harek, 'and I guess that he'll see the difference between you and the other suitors.' And now this issue was mentioned before the king, and not to make a long story of it, it was concluded that Odd would go on this expedition and collect the tribute, and if he completed his mission and got the tribute, he should marry the king's daughter, and he promised the woman with many people as witnesses.

Now Odd got ready to go, and gathered together such a troop as he wanted, and when he was ready the king saw him off. They were going by land. 'There is a costly treasure,' said the king, 'that I will give to you.'

'What is it?' said Odd. 'It's a shieldmaiden who long has followed me,' said the king, 'and has been a shield for me in every battle.' Odd smiled and said: 'It has never come to pass that women have been a shield for me, but I'll take all that you think good to offer.' The King and Odd parted now, and Odd went on until he reached a great swamp, and he crossed it with a running jump. The shield-maiden was next after him, and she became frightened when she came to the swamps. Odd asked, 'Why did you not jump after me?'

'Because I was not prepared,' she said. 'Yes,' he said, 'prepare yourself.' She hiked up her skirt and ran at the swamp a second time, and it went as before, and so the third time. Odd then jumped back over the swamps and grabbed her hand and flung her out into the swamp and said: 'Go there now, and all the trolls take you,' then jumped back over the swamps for the third time now, and awaited his men. They were all went to the end of the bog, because it was wide and hard to get across. Odd then went with his troop and sent spies before him, and they brought him news that Vidgrip had amassed a large army, and against them he marched. They met each other on a plain, and it was evening by then.

They both encamped there, and Odd kept a lookout that the evening for where Vidgrip pitched his tent. When the men had fallen asleep and all was calm and quiet, Odd stood up and walked out. He was so equipped that he had a sword in his hand and no other weapon. Soon was he there, at the tent where Vidgrip slept, and he stood there some time, and waited to see if any man would come out of the tent. It happened that a man walked out, but it was very dark. He began to speak and said, 'Why are you hiding here?' he said, 'Come into the tent or go away.'

'Yes,' he said, 'I have got myself lost. I can't find my bedroll, where I lay down early in the evening.'

'Do you know whereabouts it was in the tent?'

'I am sure that I was lying in Vidgrip's tent and one man lay in between me and him, but as it goes now, I can't find my way, but I will be every man's laughing-stock if you will not help.'

'Yes,' said the other, 'I will lead you to the bedroll that Vidgrip lies on,' and so did he. 'Yes,' said Odd, 'let's now be quiet, and all is well now, because now I see my space clearly.' Now he walked away, but Odd stood there looking after him to where he's going, until he was asleep. Then Odd stuck a peg through the tent wall where Vidgrip lay. After that he went out and went behind the tent, where that peg was. Then he lifted the tent flap and pulled Vidgrip out and cut off his head on a log. He closed the tent and let the body fall back, then he went to his tent and lay down and acted as if nothing had happened.

CHAPTER TWENTY NINE

And the next morning, when the Vikings woke up, they found Vidgrip dead and his head gone. It seemed to them such a marvel that all wondered. They now talked together, and it was decided that they take another one as leader, and call him by Vidgrip's name and have him bear the banner during the day. And now Odd woke and armoured himself. He arranged things there so that they had a standard pole erected and he set Vidgrip's head on the top of the pole. Now the two armies drew up. Odd went out before his troop and he had a much smaller force. Odd started speaking and called on the native force, and asked if they recognised the head that was borne before him. Then the people of the land thought they recognised Vidgrip's head and marvelled greatly that it could be so. Odd now gave them two choices, whether they wanted to fight against him or give up. But it seemed to them that their outlook was bleak whatever they tried, and it was advised that they yield to Odd. He took them and all these followers and went to where Odd encountered Alf Bjalki. Both had a great troop, and yet Odd had fewer than Alf. At once battle broke out between them. It was so fierce that Odd was amazed at the slaughter that happened, because he thought he saw a lot of losses from his troop. 'It follows, too,' said Odd, 'I can cut my way up to the banner of Alf, but I see him nowhere.' Then one countryman spoke, who had been with Vidgrip before: 'I am not sure,' he said, 'what's wrong with you, since you do not see him, for he goes just behind his banner and never leaves it, and this is a sign of it, that he shoots an arrow from each finger and kills a man with each one.'

'I still cannot see him,' said Odd. Then the man raised his hand above Odd's head and said: 'Look from here under my hand.'[9] And then Odd saw Alf and everything else the man had said. 'Hold it there for a while,' said Odd, and he did so. Now Odd felt for Gusir's Gifts and took one of them and put it to the string and shot at Alf Bjalki; he put up the palm of his hand, and the arrow did not want to bite. 'Now you shall all go,' said Odd, 'though none of you will suffice.' He shot all of them, but none of them bit, and then all Gusir's Gifts dropped down in the grass. 'I am not sure,' said Odd, 'but maybe it has now come to pass, what old man Jolf said, that they are now gone, Gusir's Gifts, and I will try the man's stone arrows,' and he took one of them and laid it on a string, and shot at Alf Bjalki. When he heard the whine of the arrow that flew at him, he still raised his palm, but the arrow flew through it and out of the back of his head. Odd took another and laid it to the string, and shot at Alf. He put up the other palm and meant now to protect his remaining eye, but the arrow came through that eye, into the brain, and out of the back of his head. Alf did not fall any more than before. Then Odd shot the third, and hit Alf in the waist, and now he fell dead. Now all the old man's stone arrows vanished, as he had said that they could be shot once and then they would not be found.

Now the fight was quickly over, because the enemy was routed and retreated to the city. Gydja stood there in the gate and she shot arrows from all her fingers. Now the battle died away, and everywhere the enemy troop surrendered to Odd. Near the city were shrines and temples, and Odd had them set on fire and burnt everything near the town, and then poetry came to Gydja's lips:

'Who is causing this blaze,

This battle;

Who on the other side

Uses spears?

Shrines are blazing,

Temples burn,

Who has reddened the sword edge

On Yngvi's troop?'

Now Odd answered and said this:

'Odd burns shrines

And breaks temples

And destroys

Your idols of wood;

They did no

Good in the world,

From out of the fire

They could not save themselves.'

Then she said:

'I laugh at that,

Learning what you've done

To earn Frey's anger,

His great fury,

Help me gods

And goddesses,

Aid me, Powers,

Your own Gydja.'

Then Odd said:

'I don't care

If you curse me,

Filthy woman,

With Frey's anger;

I saw your gods burn

In the blaze,

Trolls take you,

I trust God alone.'

Then she said:

'Who fostered you

To be so foolish,

That you do not want

To worship Odin?'

Then Odd said:

'Ingjald raised me

In childhood,

Who ruled Eikund

And lived in Jaederen.'

Then she said:

'I would feel rich,

I'd have enough,

If I could see

My Alf again;

I'd give sacrifices

And four estates;

And I'd fling you

Into the fire.'

Then Odd said this:

'Odd bent his bow,

Arrows flew from strings,

Jolf's work pierced

Alf right through;

I don't think he

Will accept your offer

Ravens feast

On his carcass's flesh.'

Then she said:

'Who encouraged you,

East-faring here,

A terrible journey

And treacherous?

You must have wanted

A war badly,

When you sent Alf

The fatal arrow.'

Then Odd said:

'My arrows aided me

And Jolf's work

Mighty arrows

And powerful bow;

But lastly because I

Never befriended,

Those gods you worship

I give my word.

I gave Frey

And then Odin,

Blinded both,

Thrust them in the blaze,

Off ran the gods

Away out of sight,

Anywhere a gaggle of them

Had been found.'

And again he said:

'I harried the gods

Fainthearted two,

Like goats from a fox

They ran afar;

Evil is Odin

As a close friend;

It must not continue,

Their devilish curse.'

Odd now attacked Gydja with a huge oak club. She ran away into the city with the army following her. Odd chased the fugitives, and killed everyone that he could lay hands on, but Gydja fled to the chief temple in the city, and ran inside and said this:

> *'Help me gods*
>
> *And goddesses,*
>
> *Aid me, Powers,*
>
> *Your own Gydja.'*

Odd came to the temple and would not go in after her. He went up the roof and saw where she was lying through the window. Then he took up a large stone and threw it through the window. It hit her on her spine and smashed the giantess against the stalls, and she died there. But Odd fought a battle throughout the city. He came to where Alf was; he was not yet dead. Odd then beat him with a club till he was dead. Now he gathered tribute all across the land and established the chiefs and governors. But as he says in his poem, it was in Antioch that he killed Alf and his son. And when he was done, he went away from there with great wealth and immense riches, so that no one could calculate its worth, and nothing is told of his journey until he come back to the Greek kingdom. Meanwhile it had happened in the country that King Herraud was dead, and he had been laid to rest with a mound over him. Odd at once ordered a funeral ale for him when he returned to the land, and it was prepared, then Harek betrothed to Odd his foster child Silkisif, and now at the same time the men drank the marriage ale and the funeral ale of King Herraud. And at that feast Odd was given the name of king, and he now he ruled his kingdom.

CHAPTER THIRTY

It had come to pass seven winters before that the king who ruled in Holmgard had been snatched by death, but an unknown man called Kvillanus seized the realm, and he became king there. He was somewhat strange looking because he had a mask over his face, so that no one ever saw his bare face. Men thought this strange. No one knew his family and ancestry nor land, nor where he was from. The men debated this a great deal. The news spread, and it came to Odd's ears in Greece, and it seemed to him very strange about this man, that he should never have heard about this man during all his travels. Then Odd got up in public and made a solemn vow that he should surely learn who ruled the kingdom in Holmgard in the east, and a little later he collected his forces and left home. He sent word to Sirnir, his blood-brother, and he came to meet him east of Wendland, and had thirty ships, but Odd fifty. They were all well equipped with weapons and men. They sailed eastwards to Holmgard.

Gardariki is so large a land that it contains many kingdoms. Marron was the name of one king. He ruled Moramar; this land is in Gardariki. Rodstaff was the name of a king. Radstofa was the name of where he ruled. Eddval was the name of a king. He ruled the realm that is named Sursdal. Holmgeir was the name of the king who ruled Holmgard before Kvillanus. Paltes was the name of a king. He ruled Palteskjuborg. Kaenmarr was the name of a king. He ruled Kaenugard, where the first settler was Magog son of Noah's son Japheth. All these kings now named were tributaries under King Kvillanus.

And before Odd entered Holmgard, Kvillanus had mustered troops for the previous three winters. Men thought that he had known of Odd's coming. All kings mentioned formerly were with him. Svart Geirridson was there. He was so-called after Ogmund Eythjof's Bane had disappeared. There was also a great host of Kirjalalandi and Rafestalandi, Refaland, Virlandi, Estland, Livland, Vitland, Courland, Lanland, Ermlandi and Pulinalandi. It was so great an army that no one could count it in hundreds. Men marvelled much at where this immense army should be gathered from. When Odd came ashore, he sent messengers to the king Kvillanus and challenged him to a tournament, and Kvillanus responded quickly and went to meet him with his army. He wore a mask on his face, as he was accustomed to do. But when they met, they got ready for the tournament. They had strong lances and long. They broke four lances, and they tourneyed for three days, and did not achieve anything more. Then Kvillanus said, 'It seems to me now that we've tested each other, and I think we are equal.'

'I suppose that's right,' said Odd. 'It seems to me that we understand,' said Kvillanus, 'and should fight no longer, and I will invite you to a banquet.'

'There's just one thing,' said Odd. 'What is that?' Kvillanus said. 'That,' said Odd, 'I do not know who you are, but I have made a solemn vow to learn who is king in Holmgard.' Then Kvillanus took the mask from his face and said: 'Do you know who owns this ugly head?' Odd realised that this man was Ogmund Eythjof's-Bane, because he could see all the marks he'd given him when he had torn off his beard, his face and head back to the middle of his crown. It was all healed over the bones but no hair grew. Odd said. 'No, Ogmund,' he said, 'I will never come to terms with you. You have done much harm to me, and I challenge you to fight tomorrow.' Ogmund accepted, and the day after they met in battle. It was both violent and brutal, and it there were the greatest casualties with men killed on both sides. Sirnir fought well as usual and killed many men, because Snidil bit all that was before him. Svart Geirridson turned against him, and there was a fierce battle, but

Snidil failed to bite although Svart had no armour. Svart lacked neither strength nor malice, but at the end of their duel Sirnir fell dead although with much honour. Odd killed all the tributary kings under Kvillanus, some he shot, and some he hewed down. But when he saw the fall of Sirnir, it angered him strongly, and it seemed it was happening all over again, a loss of life at the hands of Ogmund and his men. He put an arrow to the string and shot at Svart, but he put up the palm of his hand, and it would not bite. Thus went another, and the third. Then it passed through his mind that he had experienced a great loss now Gusir's Gifts were gone. He turned away from the fight and into the forest and cut himself a big club and went back into battle. But when he met Svart, they started fighting. Odd struck him with a club, not turning away till he had broken every bone in Svart and left him there dead. Kvillanus had not been idling away his time, for it is said that arrows shot out of his fingers and a man was killed by each, and with the aid of his men he had killed every man with Odd. Many had also fallen on Kvillanus' side, so that he could hardly count the dead. Odd was still up and fighting valiantly. He was neither tired nor wounded because of his shirt. Night fell upon them, and it became too dark to fight. Kvillanus then went to the city with his men who had survived. He had no more than six hundred men, all tired and wounded. He was then called Kvillanus Blaze. He ruled long in Holmgard.[10]

Odd walked off through the wilderness and woods until he came to Gaul. At that time two kings ruled, but there had been twelve realms[11]. One king was named Hjorolf, the other Hroar. They were the sons of two brothers. Hroar had killed Hjorolf's father to get the throne and he ruled the whole realm, except that Hjorolf ruled one county. Odd had come to his coast. The king was young and amused himself by shooting at targets, but it went poorly. Odd said that the shooters were bad shots. 'Could you shoot better?' said the king. 'It does not seem much to me,' said Odd, but now he shot, and always hit. Then the king made much of this man and formed a high opinion of him. The king told him how he was treated by King Hroar. Odd said he ought to request an equal division of the realms. They sent twelve men with letters to the king, and when he had read them he answered and said that it was not modest to beg such things, and that he would send them back so that no one would wish to beg such again. And then both collected men, and Odd and Hjorolf had less than a twelfth of Hroar's forces. Odd asked people to point out King Hroar. Then he took an arrow and shot at him, and hit him in the waist, and King Hroar fell there, and there was no battle. Hjorolf offered the realm to Odd, but he was not happy there long and he sneaked away overnight. Then he wandered through the woods until he came to his kingdom, and he settled there in peace. Somewhat later Kvillanus sent Odd gifts rich both in gold and silver and many precious objects and with them a message of friendship and reconciliation. Odd accepted these gifts because he was wise enough to see that Ogmund Eythjof's Bane, then called Kvillanus, was unbeatable, since he was no less a man than a wraith. And it is not written that they had further connections, and this was the end of their conflict.

CHAPTER THIRTY ONE

Odd now stayed in his country, and he had a long life there and had two sons with his wife. Asmund was named after his foster-brother, and the other was named Herraud after his mother's father, and they were both promising. One evening time when the king and queen came to bed Odd began to speak: 'There is one land where I'm going to go.'

'Where are you going?' Silkisif said. 'I'm going north to Hrafnista,' he said, 'and I want to know who holds the island, because I own it and my family.'

'I think,' she said, 'you have enough property here, you have won all Gardariki, and can take other goods and countries that you want, and I think you should not covet a small island which is useless.'

'Yes,' he said, 'it may be that the island is worth little, but I will choose the ruler it shall have, and you will not discourage me because I have decided to go, and I will only briefly be off.'

Then he sailed two ships from the land and forty people aboard each, and there is no story of his journey until he came north to Hrafnista in Norway. But the men welcomed Odd when he got there, and prepared a banquet to greet him, and they gave him a fortnight of feasting. They invited him to take over the island and all the property that belonged there. He gave back all the property and would not stay there. Then he prepared for his journey, and the people brought him fine gifts.

Odd now sailed out from Hrafnista until they came to Berurjod, which they think lay in Jaederen. Then he told his men to reef sails. Odd went ashore with his troop and came to where Ingjald's farm had been, and it was now only ruins grown over with turf. He looked over the place and then said: 'This is terrible to see, that the farm should be in ruins, instead of what was here earlier.' He then went to where he and Asmund had practiced shooting, and commented on how different the foster-brothers had been. He took them where they had gone swimming in the water, and named them every landmark. And when they had seen this, he said, 'Let us go on our way, and it won't help now to stand looking at the land, no matter what we feel about it.' Now they went down, and everywhere the ground had eroded, while it had bloomed when Odd was there before. When they went down, Odd said: 'I think now that hopes are fading that the prediction will be fulfilled, as the seeress predicted for me long ago. But what is there?' Odd said, 'what lies there, is that not a horse's skull?'

'Yes,' they said, 'and extremely old and bleached, very big and all grey outside.'

'Do you think it will be the skull of Faxi?' Odd prodded the skull with his spear shaft. The skull shifted somewhat, but then an adder slithered out and struck at Odd[12]. The snake bit his foot above the ankle, so that the venom worked at once, and the whole leg swelled up. So it took Odd so fast that they had to lead him down to the sea. And when Odd was there, he sat down and said, 'Now, split my troop in half, and forty men shall sit with me, and I will write a poem about my life, while the other forty shall make me a coffin and gather firewood. Light a fire there and burn everything up when I am dead.'

CHAPTER THIRTY TWO

Now he began the poem, while one group made the coffin and collected the wood. But those who had been chosen memorised the poem. Now Odd said this:

1st

'Listen to me warriors,

To what I will say

I give form to, speak

Now of my friends;

Too late to hide it,

Or fool yourself

No self-delusion

When fate is ruling.

2nd

I was brought up

By my father's wishes,

Fostered I was,

At Berurjod;

I was not

Unaccustomed to bliss,

Of all Ingjald

Could offer me.

3rd

We both

Spent our boyhood,

Asmund and I,

In childhood;

Shaped shafts,

Ships built,

Fletched arrows

ANONYMOUS AUTHOR

A happy time.

4th

The seeress spoke

True runes,

But I lacked the

Wisdom to obey;

I told the young

Son of Ingjald,

That I would the fields

Of my father visit.

5th

Asmund said

He would always be eager,

As long as he lived,

To follow my lead;

I said to his father,

That I would come

Back never;

Now I've broken my word.

6th

Keen to cruise

Our craft in the surf,

Was not needed

A hand to navigate;

We arrived at the island

Steep with cliffs,

There Grim owned

Great garths.

7th

They greeted me blithely,

When I came to the farm,

His men favoured me

Celebrated my coming;

I guess I might

With my friends

Exchange gold

And fair speech.

8th

It was in spring

That I learnt Sigurd

And Gudmund were going

To raid the Bjarmians;

Then I told them

Sigurd, and Gudmund,

I wished to wander

With these valiant warriors.

9th

They commanded

Warships

My two kin had them

At their behest;

Rowers wanted

To conquer,

To take the treasure

Of the Tyrfi-Finns.

10th

We approached the Bjarmian

People's bothies

Sailing in safety

Our merchant ship;

Attacked with fire

Their families;

Took as captive

The Tyrfi-Finn's serving man.

11th

He could show us,

So he said,

Where much plunder

Was to be found;

He told us to walk

Further up the way,

If we wished treasure

More to win.

12th

Bjarmian folk

Soon came to defend

Their great mound

And mustered their forces;

But they died then,

Before we left,

A number of them

Lost their lives.

13th

We left hastily

For our vessels below

Then the flight took us

Over the fen;

We found we'd lost both

Boat and sails,

Wealth and riches,

When we arrived.

14th

I quickly kindled

In thick forest

Burning fire

Upon the land,

So the flames

Keenly played

Touching the sky;

Flame burnt the timber.

15th

We saw splendid vessels,

Hasten to land

Rich-clad rowers

Racing to the shore

Glad they were,

They showed it clearly,

My kinsmen,

To greet us.

16th

Forced to leave

Our lives to fortune

Brave bold boys

In driving weather:

Seemed to carry

Sand on deck,

Our men looked for land,

Saw it not there.

17th

We arrived at an island

Beyond steep cliffs

In late summer,

Then reefed our sails;

Made haste

Most of all

To set ships on rollers

Briskly on the strand.

18th

We raised tents,

While some were

Hunting bear,

Who knew to bend bows?

On the island

We lit a good fire

Before the blaze,

Set a bear's carcass.

19th

The mountain folk claimed

They would fling us

Out of the island;

Into the waves;

We did not consider

It encouraging, hearing

ANONYMOUS AUTHOR

The promise of

The lava people.

20th

We feared them not

When we settled the islands

We weren't afraid

Of anything;

Some of us built

On the cliff above

A mighty wall;

I was one of them.

21st

I went looking

With Gusir's Gifts

Between the cliffs

And kindling flame;

I hit in the eye

One of the ettins

But in the breast

The berg-lady.

22nd

Then I got a name,

Just what I needed,

Out of the mountains

Monsters called it,

Rewarded Odd

Of the Arrows

With a fair wind

To sail away.

23rd

So we were soon ready

To sail away

From the island,

When the wind we got;

Whole we returned

Sailed back home,

So celebrated

Our family, greeting us.

24th

All warriors together

That same winter,

Glad of our gold

And good conversation;

In the spring

When the ice split

Our well-adorned vessels

We dragged to the water.

25th

We sailed off

South along the coast

All on watch

Twenty and one;

Expecting plunder,

There is for men,

If we the Elfar Skerries

Should lay waste.

26th

Found at last

Off the coast

Those two heroes,

Thord and Hjalmar;

They inquired

Which we'd rather,

Whether we wanted friendship

Or to begin the fight.

27th

Talked of treaties

Counselled together,

We thought it seemed a poor

Chance of wealth;

The band of Halogalanders

We thought best,

To join together

Seemed the better choice.

28th

We sailed our ships all

To any shore

That presented the best

Chance of booty;

Not terrified by

Any chieftains

We fought

In our warships.

29th

Raging angry

We ran into

The heroes we met

Off Holmanes;

We took

All the equipment

From those pretty boys

Of six ships.

30th

All stood

West with Skolli,

In the land where he ruled,

The people's lord;

By his enemies

We were blood-soaked,

Cut with swords,

But we seized victory.

31st

ANONYMOUS AUTHOR

The earl's warriors

Wasted the headland,

Warriors fled, pursued,

Like foxes by hounds;

Hjalmar won the fight,

Setting on fire,

With swords and damage,

Destroyed ships.

32nd

Gudmund asked

If I wished to go

Home in the autumn

And accompany him;

But I said to him,

That I would see

The north no more

Or my kinsfolk.

33rd

All agreed

To meet next summer

Eastwards at the Gautelf

And go plundering;

Hjalmar the brave

Wanted to harry

With my troops

Terrorise the southlands.

34th

They divided

Into two groups

Hardy heroes,

When the wind was good;

We sailed our ships

To the Swedish kingdom,

To visit Ingvi

ANONYMOUS AUTHOR

At Uppsala.

35th

To me gave Hjalmar

The brave

Five estates

For my own;

In my prosperity,

I took pleasure

When people offered me

Rings and peace.

36th

It was for all of us

Happy days

When Swedish warriors

And Sigurd of the north;

Plundered all

The islanders

Of their wealth,

While they felt the flame.

37th

We sailed to the west

In speeding ships

To Ireland, across

The crashing waves;

When we went there,

Women and men,

Hurried away

From out of their houses.

38th

I ran down a wide

Wagon trail,

Till I set my face

Towards the arrows;

To have back Asmund

ANONYMOUS AUTHOR

All my wealth

I would give;

All my gold.

39th

I glimpsed at last,

Where they gathered together,

Stout men

And their wives;

Where I aided four

Of Olvor's family,

Helped them lose

Their valuable lives.

40th

Called to me out of the wagon,

The elf-woman, said goodbye,

And she made me

Promise her;

Asked me to return

In the next summer,

To receive the reward

That awaited me.

41st

Unlike a byrnie

The blue rings,

Ice cold about me

Above my sides;

On my flesh

A silk shirt

Sewn with gold

Was woven close.

42nd

We left the west

Looking for plunder,

So that my men

ANONYMOUS AUTHOR

Called me coward

Until at Skida

We encountered

Evil brothers

And their death ensued.

43rd

Soti and Halfdan

At Svia Skerries

Many men

Had they murdered;

They seized,

Before we split,

Six hundred ships

Cleared stem to stern.

44th

Next we met

In our wanderings

Cunning sly fellows

At Tronuvagar;

Undoomed was Ogmund;

Of our men,

Three remained there,

But nine of his.

45th

News of killing

Could I make my boast

When we got back

To our boats;

Hjalmar and I were

Greatly dismayed

When we found Prow-Gleam

Run through.

46th

We went home from there,

Heroic boys,

The barrow of Thord

We built high;

No man dared

To go against us,

We had our way

In everything.

47th

Hjalmar and I

Each day were glad

While our warships

We did steer,

Until on Samsey

We met the fighters

Who knew well

How to wield weapons.

48th

We forced them

Under eagles' feet

Gloriless

Twelve berserks;

I suffered the death,

On that day of destiny,

The terrible loss

Of my friend.

49th

Never have I known

In all my life

A nobler man

Braver-hearted;

I bore him on my shoulders,

Hero cruel to helmets

And to Sigtuna

I took him back.

50th

I did not allow

A long wait

Before I sought Saemund

Who was at sea;

His men cleared

My ship quickly,

But myself there

I saved by swimming.

51st

I went through Gautland

Grim in mind

Six half-days passed,

Before I found Saemund;

I confronted him and his men,

Forced them to stand;

Six and eight

Faced my sword.

52nd

I went southwards over the sea

A long journey,

Till to the shallow

Creeks I went;

I walked alone,

But other

Men took

The road to Hel.

53rd

Still I came there

To Aquitania

Strong men

Ruled over cities;

Where I left four

Fallen lie,

Courageous boys;

Not where I am now come.

54th

It was in former days,

That I despatched

Messages to the north

My own folk;

I was as glad

To greet them

As the hungry

Hawk to feed.

55th

With many a mark

Of high esteem

All us three

Were honoured;

But I continued

Despite their kindness;

My brothers both

Remained back there.

56th

I travelled in haste

Away from the host,

Until I reached the spacious

City of Jerusalem;

I raced down

Into the river

And then I was clear

How Christ should be served.

57th

I recalled that

They cascaded, the waters

Of Jordan over me

Beyond the Greek empire;

Still held, however,

As I had known,

My magic shirt

All its merits.

58th

I met the vulture

Near the valley,

It flew with me

Across far countries,

Until it came

To the high crag

And let me rest

In its nest.

59th

To me Hildir

Hurried then

Glorious-framed giant,

In a rowing boat;

Let me stay

This strong fighter

Twelve months

For a rest.

60th

I help Hildir's daughter,

Huge and large,

Handsome girl,

Giant's daughter

And with her

Rather mightily,

A fine brave

Son I had

And unique among

The native people.

61st

Ogmund killed him,

ANONYMOUS AUTHOR

Eythjof's Bane

In Helluland's

Lava desert,

His nine companions,

I crushed their flesh;

Never was a Viking

Worse thought of.

62nd

Moreover he also

Slew my sworn brothers,

Sirnir and Gardar,

I snatched off his beard;

He looked unlike

Anyone at table

And was then called

Kvillanus Blaze.

63rd

Men thought me great-hearted

A gallant warrior,

When we battled

At Bravellir;

When Hroar called

For the wedge formation[13]

Odd the Wanderer

Led it into the fray.

64th

I came across two

Resolute kings

A little later,

Controlling the country;

I chose to aid

One against the other,

The young ruler

Regained his heritage.

65th

I came at last,

Where were so cocky

Sigurd and Sjolf

In that king's country;

The other noblemen

Begged me to test

My skills with theirs

In sport and shooting.

66th

I shot fewer

Than those fellows,

A subtler shaft

Was the spear in my hand;

Soon I competed

With them in swimming;

I gave them both

Bloody noses.

67th

I was set

Beside the shieldmaiden,

When to war

We went marching;

I knew that far-away

In Antioch

Men were falling,

But we grew wealthy.

68th

Felled with my sword

Many folk

And I

Whacked away;

I beat the beams

At the gate

I knocked down Bjalki,

With an oaken club.

69th

Then to me Harek

Offered comradeship,

Betrothed to me

His foster daughter;

I married Silkisif

Hilmar's daughter

Together we ruled

Righteously our realm.

70th

I wasn't allotted

Lasting bliss

For very long

As I would wish;

I could teach you

From my travels

Many lessons;

But this is the last.

71st

You must hasten

Down to the haven

We must say goodbye,

Here we part;

To Silkisif

And our sons

I send my greetings,

I'll go not there.'

And when the poem was complete, weakness quickly seized Odd, and they led him to where the coffin had been made. Odd said: 'Now all this is true, what she told me, the seeress. I will lie down in the coffin and die there. Then you shall set fire to the outside and burn everything up.' Then he lay down in the coffin, and said: 'Now you shall carry my greetings home to Silkisif and my sons and to our friends.' After that Odd died. They set fire to the wood and burnt everything up, and did not go until it was all burned. Most people say that Odd was twelve ells high, because that was the size of the coffin inside. Now Odd's comrades got ready for the journey and they travelled back east. They had a good wind until they came home. They told Silkisif the news, what had happened on their journey, and they carried her his greeting. It seemed this was sad news for her and her people, and she ruled over the kingdom after this and Harek, her foster father, with her, and held the land until Odd's sons were able to take over. Now the family line of Odd's grew up in Gardariki. But the maiden Odd had left behind in Ireland, who was named Ragnhild, had left the west along with her mother and went northwards to Hrafnista and had since married, and many people are descended from her, and her family line grew up there. And now the history of Arrow-Odd finishes, as you have now heard told.

[1] Similar sequences occur in Perrault's *Sleeping Beauty* and *The Yarn of Norna-Gest*.

[2] Comparable Viking laws appear in *The Saga of Fridthjof*, while Robin Hood is similarly chivalrous for a medieval bandit in the Middle English poem *A Gest of Robyn Hode*.

[3] Similar earth-houses appear in The Saga of the Volsungs; Chapter 17 of this saga; and the Old English poem *The Wife's Lament*.

[4] The encounter with the berserks also appears in Saxo Grammaticus' *Gesta Danorum* and *The Saga of Hervor and Heidrek*.

[5] In The Saga of Hervor and Heidrek Eyfura is a princess from Gardariki (Russia).

[6] Helluland was discovered by Leif Eiriksson at the same time as his voyage to Vinland (America). It is usually identified as Baffin Island.

[7] Known in Greek as the *aspidochelone*, a creature identical to Lyngbak appears in other stories, including those of Sinbad, St Brendan, and Pinnochio. Hafgufa later developed into the legendary Kraken, tentatively classified by Linnaeus as a cephalopod.

[8] Geirrod also appears in the Edda, where he comes into conflict with the god Thor, and in *Gesta Danorum* and various other legendary sagas.

[9] A similar method of detecting someone under a spell of invisibility is used in the *Gesta Danorum* (Book 2).

[10] These days known as Novgorod. According to the poem at the end, it was at this point that Arrow-Odd participated in the Bravic War on the side of King [Sigurd] Hring, as described in the *Gesta Danorum* (Book 8) and *Fragment of a Saga of Some Kings of the North* Chapter 8.

[11] Gaul also has twelve realms in Geoffrey of Monmouth's *Historia Regum Britanniae*.

[12] A similar prophecy and conclusion appears concerning Oleg in the *Russian Primary Chronicle*.

[13] Elsewhere Odd is said to have fought on Sigurd Hring's side, against Harald Wartooth, who was taught the wedge formation, or swine-array, by the god Odin, and used it to conquer a wide empire. When Harald saw that Sigurd Hring's men had adopted the same tactics, he saw it as evidence that Odin had now betrayed him, and doom was at hand.

VIKING LEGENDARY SAGAS

The legendary sagas, or Fornaldarsögur, are a branch of medieval Icelandic literature, a subgenre of the sagas themselves, lengthy narratives that bear a superficial similarity to modern novels; the legendary sagas concern themselves with legendary times predating the settlement on Iceland in the tenth century AD. While fantastic episodes are not unknown in sagas outside this bracket, such as Grettis Saga, and they abound in the Sagas of the Knights, (retellings of continental chivalric romances), the legendary sagas are the closest to the pagan world of Norse mythology, and also include parallels with poems such as the Old English Beowulf and the Middle High German Nibelungenlied.

The Saga Of The Volsungs: And The Yarn Of Norna-Gest

The Saga of the Volsungs was written in thirteenth century Iceland, part of a vast collection of prose stories known as the sagas. In itself, it is the product of hundreds of years of oral storytelling, and the same stories appear in the poems of the Elder Edda, another work of medieval Iceland, and also in the medieval Austrian epic poem, the Nibelungenlied, where the central character is known as Sifrid rather than Sigurd. Characters in the saga are also alluded to in the Old English poem Beowulf and they appear in Viking Age sculpture both in Scandinavia itself and also the British Isles.

The saga tells the story of a legendary family known as Volsungs, descended from the Norse god Odin, covering several generations, up until Sigurd, who slew Fafnir the Dragon and took the creature's cursed treasure, resulting not only in his death but that of everyone who owns it after him.

The story, in its various versions, became popular once more in the nineteenth century. It has inspired, directly or indirectly, writers such as William Morris and JRR Tolkien, filmmakers Fritz Lang and George Lucas, and composers and musicians from Richard Wagner, (whose Ring Cycle is the best known modern adaptation of the story), to Zodiac Mindwarp and the Love Reaction.

Now also includes The Yarn of Norna-Gest.

The Saga Of Ragnar Shaggy-Breeches:

And The Yarn Of Ragnar's Sons

Written as a kind of sequel to The Saga of the Volsungs, and following directly on from the former in some manuscripts, The Saga of Ragnar Shaggy-breeches exists in an uneasy half-and-half world between legend and history. Although some characters in The Saga of the Volsungs are based on historical persons, its central hero, Sigurd the Dragonslayer, is a mythic superhuman. Ragnar Shaggy-breeches, however, and his ambitious sons, Ivar the Boneless and his brothers, are identifiable as historical figures – although Ragnar himself is as much of a dragonslayer as Sigurd, and his sons fight even stranger monsters. The link between Sigurd and Ragnar is a little tenuous, and entirely unhistorical; Aslaug, the daughter of Sigurd and Brynhild becomes Ragnar's second wife under bizarre circumstances.

Ivar himself appears in English history as a Viking invader who killed various Anglo Saxon kings, including the St Edmund after whom Bury St Edmunds in Suffolk gets its name. In the saga, however, his transformed into a cunning trickster who uses a trick common to Germanic origin legends to become the founder of London. His father Ragnar is held to be based on a historical Viking leader who besieged Paris, while his murderer Ella is also historical – although there is no reason to believe they ever met, let alone that

Ella consigned Ragnar to death in a snake pit. It is clear that the Christian Scandinavians of the High Middle Ages, the period during which the sagas achieved their written form, were ashamed of their heathen ancestors' excesses, and Ivar's character in particular receives a whitewash. In the end, he becomes a kind of saintly figure himself, whose uncorrupted body magically guards England from invasion until William the Conqueror disinters him.

The saga itself is something of a hotchpotch, with its anonymous author apparently drawing upon writers such as the Dane Saxo Grammaticus and the Norman Dudo of San Quentin, and it has never had the literary acclaim of The Saga of the Volsungs. Nevertheless, it has been adapted on several occasions in recent decades, being the basis for the 1958 film The Vikings, and more recently the Vikings TV series. Both of these adaptations have been criticised on grounds of historic accuracy, but when their source is taken into account, with its wild and unlikely legendary narrative, they seem very sober in comparison. To do the saga justice would require the talents of more idiosyncratic filmmakers; a Ray Harryhausen, if not a Terry Gilliam, would be required to adequately realise Sibilia, the giant troll-cow whose frenzied mooing drives her enemies insane…

The Saga Of Hervor And Heidrek

The Saga of Hervor and Heidrek is the story of the sword Tyrfing, which was forged by dwarves under duress, with as many curses as blessings. Like the Rhinegold in The Saga of the Volsungs, its tale is one of tragedy and bloodshed, as it falls into the hands of owner after owner, causing chaos and mayhem as it does so.

The saga is renowned for its sequences of mystical horror, including the first Hervor's visit to the grave of her father, the undead berserk Angantyr, in which she wins back the cursed sword after a long dialogue with his ghost. This was the inspiration for the Romantic poet Anna Seward, the 'Swan of Lichfield', who based Herva, at the Tomb of Argantyr. A Runic Dialogue upon it. Another writer who found inspiration in this saga, among many others, was JRR Tolkien, who used the Riddles of Gestumblindi as one of the models for his riddle game in The Hobbit. Also of interest in the saga are the echoes it contains of real history as well as mythology; the early history of the Goths, before they left their kingdom in what is now the Ukraine to cut a bloody swathe across the declining Roman Empire. The name Tyrfing has been connected with that of the Tervingi, an early Gothic dynasty mentioned by Roman writers, and 'Gryting' with the Greutungi, another Gothic clan.

Some of the characters who appear in the later sequence are also mentioned in the Anglo Saxon poem Widsith line 115.

It has not become as famous as The Saga of the Volsungs, although it has inspired art and literature in modern times, but it has more often been used as a quarry from which other writers have extracted material. An uneven work in many ways, it nevertheless contains a great deal of interest: dwarves, magic swords and curses, warrior maidens and the undead, giants and gods, riddles and fate, all culminating in an epic battle between Goths and Huns, after which the legendary story continues into recorded history as far as the later Viking Age, linking the glorious Goths of history with the Swedish kingdom, a tradition that in many ways was revived during Sweden's imperial expansion in the seventeenth century, when, like the Goths before them, possessed by the "furor teutonicus", almost as if Tyrfing had returned, they issued forth from the womb of nations to lay waste kingdoms and empires.

The Sagas Of Ketil Trout And Grim Hairy-Cheek

The Sagas of Ketil Trout and Grim Hairy-cheek are two of the Sagas of the Men of Hrafnista, stories written in medieval Iceland about the legendary Norwegian ancestors of contemporary families. Like the rest of the Legendary Sagas, they are fantastic in tone, featuring trolls and other monsters. The Saga of Grim Hairy-cheek is in many ways a sequel to The Saga of Ketil Trout, as Grim Hairy-cheek is the son of Ketil Trout. He receives his unattractive epithet in his father's saga when his mother Hrafnhild catches sight of a hairy Lapp while conceiving him with Ketil. Ketil Trout's own nickname derives from his modesty or naivety when referring to a dragon he slays.

Ketil Trout is of a common type of hero in Norse saga, and indeed in international folklore; the 'coalbiter' or male Cinderella, who lazes by the hearth rather than taking part in domestic tasks until spurred on to adventure and heroic deeds, from which he receives 'a name that will never die beneath the heavens.' The despair of his father, considered a fool by other people on Hrafnista (modern Ramsta in Norway), he proves himself on a series of expeditions into the North where he slays dragons and fights trolls. Along the way he meets and marries Hrafnhild, daughter of Bruni, brother of the Lapp king Gusir. He slays Gusir, Bruni's rival, and obtains the magical arrows Flaug, Hremsa and Fifa and Dragvendill 'best of swords.' With these accomplishments he goes on to prove himself a hero among his own people, but he is faithless in love, and bad blood exists between his people and those of his abandoned wife Hrafnhild.

Grim Hairy-cheek inherits his father's lands and weapons, but also, it seems, something of his lucklessness in love and propensity for cohabiting with trolls. His saga is rather shorter, and episodic in nature; its most memorable episode contains elements reminiscent of Arthurian romance (the Loathly Lady motif) and later Scandinavian folklore (similar trolls appear in East of the Moon, West of the Sun). Grim himself is the father of Odd the Traveller, or Arrow-Odd, whose much longer saga is a sequel to his own story.

'And this story shall also be told.'

The Saga Of An Bow-Bender

An's Saga is about another member of the Hrafnista family that includes Ketil Trout, Grim Shaggycheek and Arrow-Odd. Chiefly set in Norway, it features almost no forays into the supernatural (although a dwarf provides An with his bow and arrows), unlike the other Sagas of the Men of Hrafnista.

An is an outlaw and archer, much like Robin Hood or William Tell, and most of his saga concerns itself with his struggle to survive in the wilds while feuding with the corrupt king Ingjald of Namdalen. Like his ancestor Ketil Trout (not to mention other legendary or semi-legendary figures such as Beowulf, Offa, and Prince Hal), An is an idle youth who goes on to prove his worth in later life. And like his kinsman Arrow-Odd, the great feud of his life ends ultimately in an uneasy truce, rather than outright victory or defeat.

An the Bow-swayer appears to be identical to Ano Sagittarius (Ano the Archer) in Book Six of Saxo Grammaticus' Gesta Danorum, although in the latter story he is no longer an outlaw feuding with a king, but a king's retainer loyal unto the death – although he remains a superlative bowman.

The Hrafnista men were claimed as ancestors by some of the more powerful families in medieval Iceland, and their supposed descendants included the troublesome Egil Skallagrimsson, a viking par excellence of the Viking Age, and even that violent, treacherous literary figure of medieval Iceland, Snorri Sturluson, author of the Edda. A later version of the saga even noted the presence of men in mid-seventeenth century Iceland who were not ashamed to claim descent from the men of Hrafnista.

The Saga Of Hrolf Kraki And His Champions

The Saga of Hrolf Kraki and his Champions is notable particularly for its links with the Old

English poem Beowulf, and it shows the close links between Anglo Saxon mythology and legend and those of the Vikings. Characters and locations are common to both the saga, a late work of the fourteenth century Icelandic literary tradition, and the poem, whose manuscript dates from the eleventh century (although it is said to have been composed in the seventh century). Both are set in Denmark and Sweden, c. 500 AD. The Hrolf of the saga is identical to the Hrothulf of the poem; the saga's Hroar is the poem's Hrothgar. Although there is no Beowulf in the saga, he has a counterpart in Bodvar Bjarki, a bear-like warrior who rescues the Danish king's hall from a monster.

However, it is also a distinct work in its own right, the culmination of a storytelling tradition, no doubt mainly in oral form, which also appears in earlier writings such as the Danish historical works of writers such as Saxo Grammaticus and Sven Aggesen. Central to the saga are the exploits of the champions of the Danish king Hrolf Kraki, a group of heroes who, like King Arthur's knights and Charlemagne's paladins, who come to outshine their liege lord, who sometimes seems an oddly mild mannered ruler. Villain of the piece is Adils, king of Sweden, comparable to the Sherriff of Nottingham in his wickedness, his theft of Hrolf's patrimony and his attempt to murder the king on his visit to the Swedish capital at Uppsala. Both this conflict and that which leads to Hrolf's downfall, the battle of Skuld, have their origins in the sins of Hrolf's father, Helgi, brother of Hroar (Beowulf's Hrothgar), a warrior in the Viking mould who rapes queens, unwittingly marries his own daughter, and later sleeps with an elf woman, whose daughter—Hrolf's half-sister—brings about the downfall of the kingdom.

As well as the magic and the mayhem of the saga, its author includes other touches. At several times characters from humble beginnings are seen triumphing over more powerful men, including the cowardly Hott, who Bodvar Bjarki, himself the son of a peasant, transforms into a fearless warrior. Another strand is the contemporary (14th century) Christian interpretation of heathen tradition; berserks are portrayed as ogre-like bullies, mainly there to be defeated by heroes; King Adils' paganism is another mark against him; and finally we are told that King Hrolf did not worship Odin—he even renounces the pagan god's gifts when he meets him in disguise—and that his only fault was that he did not know of his Creator.

It is a work of many strands, in some ways episodic, mixing pagan antiquity with Christian theology, heroism and cowardice, monsters and witches and villains. It is no surprise that in more recent times the saga has provided an inspiration to fantasy writers such as JRR Tolkien and Poul Andersen.

Sorli's Yarn: The Saga Of Hedin And Hogni

Sorli's Yarn, or The Saga of Hedin and Hogni is one of several stories found in the manuscript Flateyjarbok, a collection of stories about kings of Norway written by two Icelandic priests in the 15th century. It includes a euhemerised account of the Norse gods, followed by a version of the once famous story of the battle of Hedin and Hogni, the Hjaðningavíg, an eternal battle between two heroes brought about, in this version of the story at least, by the wiles of the god Odin, followed by an account of how one of the retainers of Olaf Tryggvason, violent evangeliser of Norway, brought an end to the curse.

The endless battle itself is a motif that also appears in the Welsh Mabinogion, where Gwynn and Nudd and Gwythyr ap Greidawl fight every May Eve until Doomsday for the hand of Creiddylad daughter of Lludd. The earliest references to a Germanic form of the legend appear in the Anglo Saxon poems Deor and Widsith, although the battle is not explicitly described. It also appears in Saxo Grammaticus' Gest Danorum, Snorri Sturluson's Prose Edda, and the Middle High German poem Kudrun, amongst other sources. In most versions the battle is endless, although in Sorli's Yarn, the power of Olaf Tryggvason and his new religion of Christianity is indicated by the ability of his follower to end to this hangover of pagan days.

The story is also notable for its references to the eponymous Sorli, who also had a longer saga to himself, The Saga of Sorli the Strong (in preparation), and to Halfdan, the protagonist of The Saga of Halfdan, Foster Son of Brana (also in preparation).

Sagas Of Ancient Kings

This is a compilation of legendary sagas that survive only in a fragmentary or reduced state. It begins with the Fragment of a Saga of Certain Ancient Kings of Denmark and Sweden, an account of the lives of such legendary conquerors as Ivar Wide-Grasp, his grandson and successor Harald Wartooth, and the latter's vanquisher and successor, Sigurd Hring, father of the more famous Ragnar Shaggy-breeches. The saga as we have it lacks both a beginning and an end, although context has been provided from other sources that relate the reigns of the same legendary kings.

The climax of the saga must be the titanic Battle of Bravellir, a legendary battle that occurred sometime before the Viking Age (its dates are notoriously uncertain), brought about when the then king of Denmark and Sweden, Harald Wartooth, in his old age, made war on his son in law Sigurd Hring. To this battle came heroes and warriors and Vikings, some of whom have sagas of their own, like Odd the Wanderer (aka Arrow Odd, whose saga is also available in this series),or Starkad the Old, whose own saga has been lost, (assuming it was ever written), but who appears like a dark shadow on the edges of other narratives. Blessed by Odin, cursed by Thor, this huge, dour warrior battled his way through lifetimes in the legendary age, and the battle of Bravellir was only one of the occasions in which he showed his strength.

Sigurd Hring was the victor at Bravellir, and after a long reign, mortally wounded in battle, he set sail in a burning ship—one of the only two 'Viking funerals' known to the sagas, the other being that of Haki. The saga breaks off, however, before this point. Where it would have gone after that remains a mystery, although the next logical step would be to relate the story of Ragnar Shaggy-breeches, whose own saga happily has survived.

Also present in this volume are three other narratives concerning legendary Scandinavian kings, traditionally linked together under the title 'Of Fornjot and his Family.' Firstly comes the story of Fornjot and his sons, Hler, Logi and Kari. Hler gave his name to the Danish isle of Laeso (Hlesey) and appears elsewhere in Norse mythology as the sea giant Aegir, husband of Ran who catches drowned sailors in her net. Logi's name means 'fire' (in the Prose Edda he bests Loki in an eating contest) and Kari is a personification of the wind. Fornjot's own name is uncertain, but it could mean 'the old giant'. They are clearly giants, and mythological personages, and their descendants are equally legendary. The same story reappears, however, at the beginning of the Saga of the Orkneymen, and this version follows the first in this volume. We conclude with the story of the kings of the Upplands (Opland in modern Sweden) descendants of that Ingjald the Ill-Advised who is mentioned in the earlier Fragment. Although this account does not mention him, the same line produced Harald Finehair, who was first king of all Norway, and whose legendary lineages take up much of the first of the three stories.

The Saga Of Half And Half's Champions

The Saga of Half and Half's Champions has some similarities with The Saga of Hrolf Kraki, and indeed with the Arthurian legends and the cycles of kings such as Charlemagne. Each tells the story of a king with a dedicated band of warriors, their heroic lives and tragic deaths. The Saga of Half differs in that the king in question is that most Norse of kings, a sea king—a man of royal birth who spurns rule on land and instead spends his life at sea, living by raiding and fighting other vikings.

An uneven tale in many ways, it takes several chapters to introduce its protagonist, telling the reader more of what came before than of Half's time as a sea king before his return to the land to meet with the plots of his stepfather. The valiant defenders in a burning hall is a motif that appears in many other sagas and poems, from the Anglo Saxon Fight at Finnsburh to the Icelandic Saga of Burnt Njal, and it would seem that this was a frequent custom in the Viking Age and earlier, for a defending force to be burnt alive in their own hall.

The saga is also notable for its weird and uncanny episodes, such as the prophecies of the merman and the well-defiler, and Geirhild's Faustian pact with Odin, the ultimate fruit of which does not appear in this saga, but in The Saga of King Gautrek. But that is another saga…

The Saga Of Thorstein Vikingsson

The Saga of Thorstein Vikingsson is a complex tale of adventure, spiced with sorcery, trollish opponents and dwarfish helpers, of curses and magical swords, of Viking raiding and romantic love matches. A long and somewhat rambling work of thrills, spills and adventures comparable to a 1930s movie serial, it acts as a prequel for the more renowned Saga of Fridthjof the Bold. It begins, like many such sagas, in a mythological landscape leavened with a scattering of euhemerisation to keep the priests happy, but rather than featuring gods like Odin the main characters in the first chapter are giants. From them comes a heroic stock whose adventures and feuds we follow through two generations.

The saga is most notable both for its fairly realistic portrayal of vikings going about their business of plundering, warring, and fighting other vikings, and its detailed accounts of the occult beliefs of the pagan Northmen. Spells for breaking free of fetters, dream interpretation, guardian spirits, berserk frenzies, magical potions, curses, trolls and dwarves, magic swords and a talking ship, Ellidi, which also features in the Saga of Fridthjof, all this and more appear. The saga as a whole is comparable with one of the more extravagant chivalric romances popular on the Continent in the Middle Ages, or the heroic fantasy of modern bookshelves.

The Saga Of Fridthjof The Bold

In the nineteenth century, and for some years into the early twentieth, The Saga of Fridthjof the Bold was one of the most famous and popular of the legendary sagas, rivalling The Saga of the Volsungs. This is doubtless due in part at least to its romantic plot; The Saga of the Volsungs is a tragic epic, ripe for adaptation into opera and film, but the romantic element (the eternal triangle of Sigurd/Gudrun/Brynhild; the incestuous love of Sigmund and Signy) is a side-line to the main plot. The forbidden love between Fridthjof and Ingibjorg is central, and is the prime cause of Fridthjof's later adventures and sufferings.

However, the saga is also of interest for its depiction of the legendary prehistory of Scandinavia, with its petty kingdoms, its pagan temples, and its bloodthirsty vikings. The temple of Balder on Sogn Fjord was long taken to be historical fact, although no evidence of its existence has yet been found by archaeologists. However, the description of this place of peace where sexual intercourse is forbidden, and the rite by which the women 'warm' the idols, seem to be echoes of genuine pagan practice, however obscure, as may be the spells of the witches who try to sink Fridthjof's magical ship Ellidi.

The first publication of the saga in Swedish translation in the eighteenth was followed by a more famous nineteenth century verse translation by Esaias Tegner, which took the European literary world by storm, and inspired other translations by writers such as William Morris and Andrew Sephton. Its influence stretched further into the realms of opera, sculpture—the cover of this volume shows the statue of Fridthjof that Kaiser Wilhelm II commissioned from Max Unger, now standing in the Sogn og Fjordan district of Norway —and various military craft were also named after the hero. Fridthjof was taken as a symbol of Germanic heroism. Perhaps it is unsurprising that after the First World War, his popularity waned considerably.

The saga is, of course, also a sequel to The Saga of Thorstein Vikingsson, which relates the adventures of Fridthjof's father and grandfather, not to mention the forefathers of the two villainous brothers Helgi and Hlafdan, and introduces elements such as the talking ship Ellidi. The deeds of the hero's descendants appear in the forthcoming Saga of Gautrek the Generous.

The Saga Of Hromund Gripsson

The Saga of Hromund Gripsson is of interest for several reasons. Firstly, an earlier version of the saga, now lost, is mentioned in another saga, the Saga of the Sturlungs, a long saga about Snorri Sturluson's family, where Sverri, king of Norway, finds Hrolf of Skalmarnes' account of 'Hrongvid the Viking and Olaf King of Warriors, and the howe-breaking of Thrain the Berserker, and Hromund Gripsson' to be 'amusing' and says that he finds such 'lying sagas' the most entertaining.

The saga as we have it is a later version, based not on Hrolf of Skalmarnes' lost work but on the later Griplur, a rima (rhyming poem) that retells the earlier tale.

Also of interest is Thrain's sword Mistiletein ('Mistletoe'), whose name is reminiscent of the story of the Death of Baldur, slain by a spear of Mistletoe, in Snorri's version, or by a sword (nameless) in Saxo Grammaticus' account.

The saga's hero, Hromund Gripsson, is descended from Hrok the Black, who appears in The Saga of Half and Half's Champions. Fighting valiantly for his king, Olaf, he makes enemies as well as achieving notable victories. Hrongvid the Viking's brother is one Helgi the Valiant, who seems to represent the Helgi who appears, in more than one incarnation, in three Eddic poems. It is said in one of the poems that he was later reincarnated a third time, and with him his Valkyrie lover, Kara, who also appears in this saga, although both are antagonists. There is also an episode in which Hromund hides from his enemies, which is very close to one of the adventures of the second Helgi, Hundingsbane.

Finally, of interest, is the mysterious figure of Blind the Evil, who seems to represent a highly unsympathetic form of the god Odin, although it seems that the writer of the saga fails to appreciate this.

The saga is fairly uneven, although as entertaining as King Sverri said of Hrolf of Skalmarnes' version, and not of the highest quality, but it is of great interest for what it represents: the lost sagas of the North, which may one day be rediscovered. Until then, we have The Saga of Hromund Gripsson.

The Saga Of Asmund, Bane Of Champions

The Saga of Asmund, Bane of Champions is one version of a story that appears throughout Germanic tradition and indeed has analogues as far flung as Ireland and Persia. The earliest surviving version in a Germanic language is the Old High German Hildebrandslied. Although much of this manuscript is missing, it tells the tale of a duel between two kinsmen, Hildebrand and Hadubrand, who are initially unaware of their family connections, one of whom is a champion of the Huns. Frustratingly, the text breaks off before the resolution of their combat. In the Hildebrandslied, and various other versions of the same story, the fighters are father and son, and the usual tragic conclusion is that the father kills his own son.

This saga is unusual in that the two kinsmen are brothers, rather than father and son, but the tragic conclusion is retained, as is the name Hildibrand, in its Old Icelandic form. However, elements of The Saga of Heidrek the Wise are also included, with the cursed swords forged by supernatural smiths under compulsion from an unwise king, and the tragic conclusion is seen as the workings of this curse. Although it varies with a number of other versions of the story (such as an episode in the Thidrekssaga, the Irish 'Death of Aoife's Only Son' and the Persian Shanameh with the fight between Sohrab and Rustam), it is almost identical to a story contained in Saxo Grammaticus' Gesta Danorum, where the main difference lies in the names of the combatants, Halfdan and Hildiger.

The Saga Of Sturlaug The Hardworking

The Saga of Sturlaug the Hardworking is one of the longer legendary sagas. Set in the early days of the legendary history of the Northlands, when Frey still ruled over Sweden, the action centres initially on Trondheim in Norway before moving to more exotic realms to the north and east, some locations real, others, such as Hundingjaland, pure fantasy, originating in travellers' tales from the classical and medieval periods.

Its hero, Sturlaug, gains his epithet when he is presented with a particularly difficult quest—to find the horn of the aurochs—by a villainous king who is also Sturlaug's rival in love. With the aid of his sworn brothers, with whom he grew up, our hero sets out on this and several other wild and weird quests, encountering trolls, monsters, and sorcerers, with elements drawn from saga tradition, medieval geography, and even natural history. And like The Saga of Thorstein Vikingsson, this long tale is a kind of prologue the story of the hero's son, in this case Hrolf the Ganger, whose own fantastic adventures will soon follow.

The Saga Of Hrolf The Ganger

The Saga of Hrolf the Ganger is one of the most entertaining and fantastic of the legendary sagas. It is notable not only for a plot that contains more elves, dwarfs, berserkers, trolls, giants, undead kings, witch-lords, warriors, wizards, treachery and sorcery than most novels in the modern fantasy genre, but also for its engaging narrator, a time-served storyteller better able than many public speakers at coping with hecklers, pedants, and amateur literary critics. It provides a fascinating insight into the original context of storytelling in which these sagas had their origin.

Despite the title, and the name of its eponymous hero, the saga has no connection with the semi legendary founder of Normandy. Instead, it is a sequel of sorts to The Saga of Sturlaug the Hard-working, (also available in this series), quite clearly by another hand, although its author has a similar fascination with geography and other disciplines. This Hrolf, who lives long before the Viking Age, in that legendary time a generation after Odin and his fellow gods founded dynasties in the Northlands, is a 'coal-biter' or unpromising anti-hero, whose adventures take him to Denmark, Russia, and finally England, but never Normandy or the Frankish kingdom. His foes are an unruly crew of villainous Vikings, berserkers and trolls, treacherous peasants and dwarfs, while his friends include valiant warriors, wonder-horses, and beautiful princesses.

His adventures are many and unlikely, although their entertainment value is matched by the passages in which the narrator breaks the fourth wall to take to task those killjoys in the backrow whose heckling and hair-splitting is ruining a damn' good story.

The Saga Of Bosi And Herruad

https://www.amazon.com/gp/product/B09C6NPZ3M?ref_=dbs_m_mng_rwt_calw_tkin_16&storeType=ebooks

Printed in Great Britain
by Amazon